THE
MESSENGERS

THE
MESSENGERS

EDWARD HOGAN

CANDLEWICK PRESS

Copyright © 2013 by Edward Hogan

First U.S. edition 2015

Library of Congress Catalog Card Number 2014939364
ISBN 978-0-7636-7112-9

15 16 17 18 19 20 BVG 10 9 8 7 6 5 4 3 2 1

Printed in Berryville, VA, U.S.A.

This book was typeset in Cambria.

Candlewick Press
99 Dover Street
Somerville, Massachusetts 02144

visit us at www.candlewick.com

To Blake

ONE

We're drawn to each other, us messengers. We must be. I remember the first time I saw him, down by the beach huts. There was something about him. The *look* of him. How could I not go over?

You might even say it was fate, but I don't believe in that.

I'd been sent to Helmstown for a little break. Back home, there'd been all sorts of trouble. My brother, Johnny, had punched an off-duty policeman during a pub brawl, and the guy was in intensive care. A few days later, some shady characters had thrown a brick through the window of our flat. Johnny, scared about what the police might do to him, was on the run. Mum had gone to stay with her boyfriend (who I don't like), so she'd given me some cash and sent me down to the coast to stay with my aunt and uncle and my cousin, Max. It was the summer holidays.

My name is Frances, but they called me *"Fraaaaancers"* in Helmstown, because of the accent. It was like a different name, and Helmstown was like a different world.

So there we were, me and Max, walking the path above the seawall as the night came down. The day had been muggy, but the wind was fresh now, and when it came off the sea, you felt like you'd been slapped. The beach huts were on our left, and almost all of them were dark and padlocked. They looked like cold little men in hats.

"Where are these mates of yours, then, Maxi?"

"By the Coffee Shack probably," he said.

The Coffee Shack! Back home, we didn't meet our friends for *coffee* after dark.

Max was a year younger than me, and the last time I'd seen him, he'd been a chubby little boy in shorts who collected beetles and watched cartoons. He'd had a growth spurt since then. Now he swished his hair to one side and wore geek-chic thick-rimmed glasses with thin lenses and low-rise skinny jeans with the bum hanging down. He carried a skateboard. It was nice: I'd turned up expecting a little squirt to hang out with, and I'd found a proper friend. Maybe.

Farther up the path, I could see that one of the beach huts was lit from the inside. Lamplight spilled out beyond the open red door.

"So, what did the doctor say about your fainting? You're hardly a delicate flower, Frances," Max said.

"He said it was your mum's cooking," I said.

It wasn't. Auntie Lizzie's a great cook. The truth was I'd been having these funny turns for a while. The Helmstown doctor was as clueless as the doctors back home. It was a mystery. Basically, every now and then I had a blackout.

What the doctors didn't know — because I never told anyone — was that when I woke up, in a daze, I started drawing.

I liked to draw in normal life. I kept a little sketch pad and a tin of Berol Venus green cracked-varnish pencils. In normal life, I drew what I'd been taught to draw: bowls of fruit, a knackered trainer, a collection of glass bottles. Typical art class stuff.

But the drawings I did after these blackouts were different. Usually they were just a jumble of geometric shapes or swirls. They were crazy, more like the slides our art teacher showed us of the paintings of Pablo Picasso and his mates. Except my drawings made less sense. In fact, until that morning at Auntie Lizzie's, the drawings had never made *any* sense. Until then, they'd just been random scribbles, incomplete pictures. Of course, the reason I never told anyone about the drawings was because I didn't fancy being locked away in a mental institution.

Recently the blackouts had started to get more regular. They used to happen about once a year, but now it was more like once a month. The doctors thought it was to do with my period. They thought I was anemic.

Anyway, I'd blacked out in my auntie's kitchen that morning. The usual: tiredness, a smell of smoke, colors going weak, and then the world closing in from the sides. I fell off my chair, which probably looked quite dramatic. Auntie Lizzie took me up to my room, and — when she'd gone — I did my drawing, still in a strange sort of trance.

But this time, the drawing made sense. The sketch contained

people, buildings. It was a street scene. A place I recognized. The clarity of the image was amazing. It was still my style, but way more sophisticated. Like a photograph, almost. And what the drawing showed . . . well, I didn't want to think about it.

As we got closer to the open beach hut, a man stepped out, long and lean. His face was calm as he smoked. His jaw was strong, the lips thick as they blew. He wore dusty, sand-colored workman's boots, jeans with paint stains, and a tracksuit top with the sleeves rolled up. His hair was blond and cut tight to his head. He was oldish; late twenties. The unusual thing about him was that he had a small magnifying glass above his right eye — the kind jewelers use to study diamonds — with a strap around his head to keep it in place.

I couldn't stop looking at him. It's difficult to explain why, to separate all the feelings. Thinking back, perhaps I recognized something in him. There was an attraction, too, although I might not have admitted it at the time. His body seemed to be wound tight with power, and I found myself staring at the wiry muscles in his lower arm. He took a draw on his cigarette and adjusted the magnifying glass on his forehead. Then he nodded to me as we passed, like he knew me, as if he were thinking the same things I was.

I looked back and took in the interior of the beach hut behind him, lit up by a big desk lamp. I could only see a fragment from that angle, but there were paints and brushes in cups, and daubs of color everywhere. We walked on, me and Max. My heart beat fast, but I tried to laugh it off. "Did you see that guy?" I said. "What did he have on his head?"

"No idea," Max said. "He sells postcards, I think."

"You know him?"

Max looked at me, surprised by the questions. "No," he said. "I've just seen him around."

I shot one last glance over my shoulder, but the man had gone back into the hut, and his fag end was rolling on the concrete of the path, the tip like a hot grain of sand.

It was almost completely dark when we saw the group of boys huddled by the light of the Coffee Shack, a small building with a serving hatch that backed onto the beach. A man was walking away from the Shack with a coffee in one hand and a slim dog held on a lead in the other. The boys behind him had skateboards. One of their phones glowed white.

"Are they your friends?"

"Yeah," Max said.

Suddenly I didn't feel like being in a crowd. "I think I'm going to head back to the house, Maxi," I said.

"They're not *that* bad," Max said with a grin.

"It's not that. I'm just a bit tired, you know."

"Be careful," he said.

"You southerners are all soft."

Max laughed. He put down his board and rode toward his mates, and I went the other way.

I knew where I was going, and it wasn't back to the house.

TWO

The door of the hut was still open, but he was bent over his work now, the magnifying glass pulled down over one eye. I stood back from the entrance for a moment and took in the tiny heater and the round mirror that reflected the sea, the swaying masts of the boats by the beach, and the dark shape of me. There was a postcard rack behind his chair and a hand-painted postcard on his desk, but he wasn't painting. He was studying it. From the angle I was at, I couldn't see the detail.

He must have noticed my shadow because he looked up, his free eye still closed. I imagined how I must have seemed to him through the magnifying glass: warped and blurred and massive.

"You're back," he said. He had a faded accent. Scottish or Irish. "I thought you might be."

"Did you?" I said. "Maybe in your mind, this kind of hovel is a girl magnet." I tended to lash out a bit when nervous.

He shrugged and I was surprised to see that I'd upset him. He turned back to the postcard and muttered something.

"Anyway, I was just passing and I saw your postcards," I said. That was a lie, and the look on his face told me that he knew as much. "Do you paint them?"

"Some of them."

"Can I buy one to send to my mum?"

"Sure. Anything on the rack is fifty p."

Without stepping into the hut, I eyed the postcards on the rack. They were just the usual rubbish. Seafront scenes, beach huts, pictures of Princess Di, cartoons of vicars ogling women with big boobs.

"I wanted one of the hand-painted ones."

He sighed and took off the magnifying glass. "I don't think you do."

"What do you mean?"

"It doesn't matter. We'll get to that later."

His manner was businesslike, as if it was just inevitable that our conversation would continue.

"Who said anything about later." I stepped away from the door and looked down the path, but there was nobody about. The sea fizzed as it dragged over the stones. I stared out on the endless darkness. You didn't get that sort of dark stretch back home.

"I've seen you around," he said.

"I doubt it. I've only been here a week."

"Please yourself."

"I generally do. What, you think you're a mystic? Some sort of fortune-teller?"

"I'm not a mystic," he said.

"Not in that tracksuit top, you're not. Is that supposed to be retro?"

He laughed. "No. I probably bought it the first time it was fashionable. I just wear it to work in. It helps me to create a distance from what I have to do. It's why I come here. Different place, different clothes. It's not the kind of work you want to take home with you."

"It all sounds a bit serious for selling postcards."

"I'm talking about my real work."

There was a look about him when he said that — somewhere between frightened and lethal.

"What am I doing here?" I said under my breath.

"You couldn't help it."

He stood up out of his chair. He was long and tight as a guitar string. He turned over the postcard on his desk and wrote something on the back in pencil. "Do you really want to see one of the hand-painted postcards?" he said.

"I don't know," I said, glancing at the card. "Not if you've written your number on it."

He smiled for a moment, then suddenly stopped. "I don't need to. You'll be back. Listen, you go past Friston Street, don't you, on your way home? Will you post this for me? It's very important."

"You're not clever," I said. "I'd have to walk past Friston Street to get anywhere."

"Fine. But will you deliver it?"

He gave me the postcard. I didn't look at it. "Why should I?" I said.

"How are you feeling?" he said, ignoring my question. "After this morning? Eh? Drained, I bet. It drains you, doesn't it?"

"What are you talking about?"

"You had an attack, didn't you? This morning? A blackout. I can tell, because you're just getting your color back. What did you draw afterward?"

I shook my head and turned to go. "Bugger off, you freak," I said.

"My name's Peter Kennedy," he said. "Pete."

"Bugger off, *Pete*," I said.

I began to walk away, and then I turned back. He was standing in the doorway of the hut, the light spilling out around him. "I'm Frances Clayton," I said. I don't know what came over me.

"OK," he said, "I'll probably speak to you tomorrow."

"What makes you think that?" I said.

"You'll need to talk," he said, and pulled the door shut.

Friston Street was long and quiet. The blossom petals had fallen to rot on the pavement, and the houses looked pale orange in the streetlight. I stopped beneath one of those streetlights and examined the postcard. I shuddered, but I didn't know why.

He was a talented painter; that much was clear. It was so lifelike, I had to check that the people in it weren't moving. There was nothing particularly interesting about the subject of the postcard, but the detail — for something so small — was astonishing, and I knew now why he'd been using that little magnifying glass to study it. This was the scene:

A street, with grand white houses on either side.

The sea, at the end of the street.

A thin woman carrying a big box across the road.

A man looking out of the open second-floor window of one of the houses.

A traffic warden studying a white van.

A blue car, parked at a strange angle behind one of the nice black streetlamps they had on those old Helmstown roads.

A weird, uncanny feeling came over me. I felt sick looking at the painting, but I figured that was what happened when you studied something so small. I'd had a long day.

On the back of the postcard, there was no message, just a name and address, in Peter Kennedy's surprisingly neat handwriting: *Mr. Samuel Richard Newman, Flat 3, 14 Friston Street, Helmstown, HM4 4TN.* Nothing else.

Suddenly I wanted the thing out of my hands, so I ran up to the door of number 14, dropped it through the letterbox, and carried on down Friston Street, thinking of Peter Kennedy.

I felt a hand on my shoulder and I spun round, gasping. It was Max.

"Bloody hell, Maxi! Don't creep up on people like that."

"I thought you'd gone home ages ago," he said.

"No, I . . . I just went for a bit of a stroll."

"Are you OK?" he asked. People kept asking me that, because of my blackouts and the mess back home. The truth was I felt like I was coping fine. But I didn't know what was coming, did I?

THREE

I couldn't sleep that night. It wasn't so much because of my strange meeting with the man in the beach hut or the drawing I'd done after my blackout — although I'd been so freaked out by the sketch, I'd buried it in my kit bag. Recently when I couldn't sleep, it was because I didn't know where my brother was.

So, yes, he'd got into a stupid argument outside a pub and punched an off-duty policeman. Johnny was a boxer and that's just the way he'd been rewired, through his training. Witnesses said the police officer was unconscious before he hit the ground, and because of this, he didn't put his hands out to break his fall, so his head snapped back against the pavement. That's what did the damage.

The time it takes a professional boxer to throw a punch is one-tenth of a second. That's how long you've got to get out of the way. That's how long it takes to split two lives in half.

Staying in Helmstown, along with this new development in my fainting fits, reminded me of the first time I'd seen Johnny fight. That was also the first time I blacked out. The junior championship bout was taking place at the Hilton Hotel on the Helmstown seafront, on a scalding hot day in August. I was five years old when me and Mum traveled down to watch. Too young, really, for something like that.

Johnny was a youth boxing sensation, and our granddad had high hopes for him. He had a chin of steel, Granddad said. As a little girl, I had once stroked his face and said, "Your chin isn't made of steel."

"It's just a thing folk say," Johnny had answered. "It means I can take loads of punches."

"Why would you want to do that?" I'd said.

Even before watching my first fight, I'd seen how our house changed in the days before one. It was all about trying to get Johnny's weight down. He'd weigh himself twelve times before lunch. He'd ditch the steak-and-egg breakfasts he ate when he was training and the milk shakes that made his farts smell and were named after natural disasters: Cyclone, Whirlwind. He'd replace all that food with . . . nothing. Well, sometimes he'd chew a whole pack of Hubba Bubba and walk around the neighborhood, spitting, because he thought if he could get rid of all his spit, he'd drop a couple of pounds.

Granddad would come and stay with us, and everyone would wake up early and play loud and ridiculous music. In the evenings, we would go to bed when it was still light, but Johnny wasn't allowed to come to my room and tell me stories. I would wake to the sound of the bathroom scales whirring. I loved Johnny and I didn't want there to be less of him.

It was as if all of the pipes and cables in the house fed into and out of my brother. As we got nearer to the day of the fight, Mum would become tense and shout at me for nothing, but Johnny would tell me it was going to be OK. "I don't worry about getting hit, Fran," he said once. "The worst thing, for me, is having to take my top off in front of all those people."

There was a fashion, at that time, of giving boxers nicknames from retro films, and they decided to call him Johnny "Top Gun" Clayton.

The seafront was packed on the day of that Helmstown fight. Not many Claytons had been to a Hilton, and me and Mum felt out of place. Auntie Lizzie hadn't moved to Helmstown yet, and we were staying at Nana and Granddad's funny little house, just down the coastal road in Whiteslade. So it was odd to walk through the posh, cool corridors of the Hilton and then into this rowdy, darkened ballroom that stank of sweat and cigarette smoke. They'd built a mini grandstand for the spectators to sit in. I remember how the backs of my thighs stuck to the blue folding seats and how the ring, which was so brightly lit, looked like a square swimming pool. I remember thinking that the announcer looked odd standing in the boxing ring in his suit and bow tie. And I remember Mum, with her hair dyed red and her white shirt, as still and straight as the lion statues outside big old buildings.

The theme from *Top Gun* played as Johnny climbed through the ropes, and he wore big reflective aviator sunglasses like they did in the film. Granddad slapped him on the back and took off his glasses. Johnny opened his mouth wide and stuck his tongue out — a little habit he had. I tapped Mum and did an impression of him. She smiled weakly.

Granddad tightened the straps on Johnny's head guard, took the knotted towel from around his neck, and then tied his bootlaces. That's when I started to get worried. How was Johnny going to win a fight if he couldn't even tie his laces?

The other lad was tall and strong. He looked like a man, really. His name was Gary "Basher" Bradley. I felt like you do when you get on a theme-park ride and the wheels start to turn, and you know you've made a terrible mistake. When the bell went to signal the start of the first round, the men in front of us stood up, so I couldn't see. They were cheering for the other guy. "Kill him, Bash!" "Do him!" "Go-o-o on, Basher!" they shouted.

Mum didn't bother to stand. She just stared into the backs of these men. I climbed on my chair and peered over.

I didn't know anything about boxing, but I learned quickly, and I didn't need anyone to tell me Johnny was losing. Basher Bradley had him in the corner of the ring and was pounding him in the stomach. To my relief, Johnny danced away from him and shrugged. He smiled, as if to say, "Is that all you've got?" Typical Johnny.

But Bradley had more.

Johnny was trying to protect his stomach, and Bradley landed a right cross (I know all the names of the punches now) on Johnny's chin of steel. Several things were horrible to me. The first was that Johnny's gum shield shot out and skidded across the ring. I didn't know he was wearing a gum shield — I didn't know what a gum shield *was* — so I thought a piece of Johnny's jaw had been chipped off. I was too upset to scream. I couldn't even turn away. When you watch a boxing match, you feel like you're taking part, especially if someone's getting a beating. And in some ways, just by being there, just by watching it happen, you *are* taking part, aren't you?

Anyway, the worst thing about it was that Johnny didn't go down. He stayed on his feet for another two rounds and took all sorts of punishment. I was the one, in fact, who hit the floor. I caught a whiff of smoke, and the last thing I remember was looking up at the ceiling, beyond Mum, beyond the fat men who were throwing air punches of their own. The ceiling had fancy swirling borders and a chandelier hanging like a bunch of flowers.

During the weeks I spent in Helmstown at Auntie Lizzie's, I kept thinking back to that day, the fight, and that first blackout. The memories kept intruding: waking up in the bedroom of my Nana and Granddad's house in Whiteslade; Johnny standing over the bed; the trancelike state I was in; and the sudden urge to draw. I suppose it was natural that I would remember my first blackout so clearly. After all, it changed my life.

With no chance of getting any sleep, I decided I might as well get up and do something semi-constructive. It was pointless, lying there just *thinking* about Johnny.

I always had the hope, especially late at night, that he might have found his way to an Internet café and e-mailed to say he was safe. At around one a.m., I left the spare room and crept around Auntie Lizzie's big house. It was beautiful, all dark wooden floors and clean cream walls. Books everywhere. It was a world apart from our flat back home. Auntie Lizzie had married Robert, an architect who had his own practice, whereas my mum had married — well — my *dad*, who I'd never even met. "Don't screw your life up for love," Mum had always told us.

Our flat was so small, you could barely breathe without waking someone up, but here, there was space and privacy. I sneaked up to the top floor, into Uncle Robert's study, and turned on his iMac. While I waited for it to fire up, I looked out the window. A black cat with white socks slinked along a low wall outside a house across the street. I'd seen the cat before. It was the one I'd drawn after my last blackout. It looked up at me now, its eyes lit with the reflection from the streetlight. Accusing me. I shuddered and closed the curtains.

There was no message from Johnny, and I didn't know what to do anymore. I'd called all the guesthouses and B&Bs back home, and the few friends that Johnny had, but they were quick to distance themselves from him now. I'd called them cowards.

I Googled Johnny and tried not to read the old news reports. There was no further information, so I went on Facebook and checked up on my friends back home. Keisha, my best mate, had updated her status four hours earlier:

Keisha McKenzie misses Frances Clayton.

I commented that I missed her, too, and wrote that Helmstown wasn't as bad as I thought it would be. I spent a bit of time looking at the pictures from a recent party and felt annoyed that I was missing out on the summer holidays — the time when everybody had those life-changing experiences — but what could I do?

I checked my e-mails one last time. There was still nothing from Johnny, only a single unread message from someone called P. Kennedy. Junk. Then it hit me. The man from the beach hut. How did he get my e-mail address?

I don't know if I can handle this, I thought. But I knew I wouldn't be able to sleep until I'd read what he had to say. I opened the e-mail.

It was a short message, with a link:

Dear Frances Clayton,

Be here at 11 a.m. tomorrow and you will begin to understand. I know you think I am strange, but if I am, then so are you. I want to help.

Regards,

Peter Kennedy

I clicked the link, and it took me to a map. The map showed a network of streets in Helmstown, near the seafront. Halfway along one of the streets, Landsmere Road, was a red pushpin.

I didn't write the address down, and I tried to forget the time. But I knew I would remember both of them, and I knew I would be there. Peter Kennedy flashed into my mind, bits of him. His lips, the workman's boots, the streaks of paint on his long fingers. I had spoken to him only for a few minutes, but I couldn't get him out of my head. It was a raw, dangerous sort of feeling.

I updated my Facebook status:

Frances Clayton is in a right state.

FOUR

I didn't wake up until 10:30, when I heard music downstairs. I threw on some jeans and a top, and went down to the kitchen, where Auntie Lizzie was dancing to Lady Gaga. I'd always thought of Auntie Lizzie as a bit of a style icon. Her hair was light brown, smooth and bobbed, like a better version of mine. She wore elegant glasses, wide-legged trousers, and a soft camel-colored sweater. "Babycakes!" she shouted when she saw me. She grabbed my hands and started moving me to the beat. I tried to pretend that I was too tired for dancing, but I couldn't stop myself from grinning.

Uncle Robert was sitting in the corner, nodding to the beat and drinking coffee from a tiny cup. Robert was a good guy, but he was one of those Helmstown dads who thinks he's down with the kids. He had stubble, wore hoodies, and had longish gray hair, which was supposed to look wild, but I knew he had it trimmed every fortnight. He was into Italian food and fashion: espressos and expensive loafers with no socks. He said "hey" instead of hello.

"Morning, Uncle Robert," I said.

"Hey," he said.

"You not working today?"

"No. I'm taking a day off."

"Getting your hair cut?" I said. Uncle Robert smiled. He pretended to like my sass, but I could tell it made him a bit uncomfortable.

"Actually I thought it might be nice if we all went out to the Downs. There's a few good hikes. We thought you should get some fresh air."

"Can't do it, sorry," I said. "I've got to meet someone."

"Oh, right," said Uncle Robert. "That's nice. Who is it?"

"Robert!" said Auntie Lizzie. "Don't pry."

"I'm only taking an interest, Liz. Besides, Frances is staying in our house, and we always tell each other where we're going."

The old *we* trick. *We* do this, *we* do that, *we*'re part of a team. Uncle Robert and Auntie Lizzie weren't exactly strict, but they had their rules and boundaries, and I reckoned Robert worried that I might lead Max astray.

"Come on, Fran, cough it up!" said Uncle Robert, smiling. "Where are you off to?"

"I'm going to one of those little beach huts to meet a suspicious-looking older man."

"Ha-ha," Uncle Robert said. "You're very droll."

I turned back to Auntie Lizzie, who was still lightly holding one of my hands. "Did Mum call?" I asked.

"No, Fran," Auntie Lizzie said. "But sometimes I miss the phone."

20

"Especially when it doesn't ring," I said. "Anyway, I've got to go."

"You could call *her*, you know, Frances," Auntie Lizzie said.

"I've tried. She doesn't want to talk to me."

Auntie Lizzie winced. "Do you want me to wash anything for you? I could unpack your bags, hang up the rest of your clothes," she said.

"No," I said sharply, thinking of the drawing at the bottom of my kit bag. I calmed my voice. "That's very kind, Auntie Lizzie, but I'll be fine."

I put my shoes on and walked out the door. The black cat with white socks stood on the low wall across the road. An old woman, who must have been its owner, shuffled down her path and stroked it. But the cat was looking at me. Looking daggers.

I have a bad sense of direction, so I had to use the map on my phone to find Landsmere Road. Standing at the top of the street, I was overtaken by the sensation that I'd been there before. The sunlight was weak and turned the big white houses a lemony color. The street funneled down toward the sea, which cut the sky in half. Sometimes, in Helmstown, the sea appeared to be as tall as a building. It loomed in the background in a way that I found unsettling. Peter Kennedy was nowhere to be seen, and I thought about leaving.

A car pulled up to my left, and a woman got out. I recognized her vaguely — the thin arms, the blond plaited hair. Then it clicked. The woman was from the postcard. I looked around. I was standing on the street that Peter Kennedy had painted. I began to feel a little queasy, but I didn't start to really freak out until the woman opened the trunk of her car and hefted a big box onto her thigh.

"No," I said to myself. "This is stupid. It can't be."

Then the traffic warden ambled around the corner, checking his little handheld machine.

Up above, there was the noise of a man unlocking one of the flaky old windows on the top floor of a whitewashed house.

The image from the postcard was slowly emerging into real life. And it was almost complete. I wanted to leave, but I couldn't. I felt as if I were making it all happen somehow, although I couldn't do a thing about it. I could barely even move.

The man leaned over his windowsill, lighting the cigarette.

The traffic warden stopped by the white van to examine the parking permit in the window.

The thin woman with the plaited hair hauled the box a little higher and began to struggle across the road, and with one last act, the scene that I remembered from Peter Kennedy's postcard came together:

A blue car swerved from the main road into the street and smacked the lamppost at speed, the bonnet crumpling around it like a grasping fist.

I was already running. I could not speak or call out. All I could hear was my own breathing, loud and frantic. The thin woman dropped her box, and books skidded across the road.

A man came out of one of the houses and ran down the steps from his door. "I'm a doctor," he said to the other people in the street, who were moving toward the car. "I've called an ambulance."

I stopped a few meters from the front of the car and stared through the windscreen. The driver was motionless, his head resting on his shoulder in a way that didn't look right. I managed to gasp out some words. "I think it's too late."

The doctor stopped and frowned at me. Then he turned back to the car. He opened the door, and the driver's arm slipped out. The doctor crouched down and held the driver's wrist, checking for a pulse.

The doctor slowly bowed his head.

"This can't be happening," I whispered to myself, waiting for a sudden wave of nausea to pass as a crowd gathered around the car. I tried to track back. An image of Peter Kennedy's face came to me, half bright in the light from his desk lamp. *You will need to talk*, he had said after giving me the postcard. Thinking of those words, I was flooded with anger. He knew. Somehow, he knew. I didn't know what was going on, and I wanted to dismiss the whole thing as some kind of prank. But the man in the car was real. And he was dead. I straightened myself up and started walking toward the seafront. Then I began to run.

It had been a long time since I had run so fast and with such fury. The sea rose up, its horizon not wavy, but a hard ruled line. I sprinted past the big white houses and the pretty lawns, the Coffee Shack and the skateboarders, the noise of sirens already ringing out. A man with a gray whippet and a takeaway coffee stumbled out of my way. I ran until I reached the beach huts, which were colorful in the daylight, bright and sickly.

FIVE

His beach hut was closed and locked, but I could smell recent cigarette smoke. I knocked. Nothing. I wasn't in the mood to wait. I wanted answers. Stones from the beach had spilled onto the path. I picked some up and hurled one at the door.

"Jesus!" he shouted from inside. I heard something topple over. *Good*, I thought.

"You're in there, I take it?" I shouted. I cocked my arm, ready to throw the next stone.

"Just a minute, for God's sake," he said.

He opened the door and raised his arm to his face, thinking I was going to throw the stone. I dropped it and he relaxed.

"You owe me an explanation," I said.

"Look, come inside, will you?"

"No way. You're in no position to tell me what to do."

He straightened up. I felt the power shift in his favor. "I think I am," he said.

I paused and closed my eyes. In my mind, I saw the driver of the car with his head on his shoulder.

"He's dead. That man is dead," I said. The reality was only just hitting me.

"Come inside."

I had to stop myself from shaking. "What's going on?" I said. I squeezed into his hut, and he locked the door, muffling the noise of the sea as surely as if he'd put his hand over its mouth.

Peter sat in a chair, looking up at me. The sleep-mode light of a closed laptop blinked in the corner.

"At least tell me who he was," I said. "Because you *know*, don't you?"

"He was Samuel Richard Newman, and it was his time."

Samuel Richard Newman. The name from the postcard.

"You knew. I don't know how, but you knew what was going to happen. And you made me watch it. I could report you."

He looked at me sadly. His stubble was blond, like little splinters of light wood, and his eyes were green and bright in the gloom of the hut, like they'd soaked up the light from the sun outside. "Report me to whom?" he said.

"The police. I could call the police," I said.

He sighed as if he felt sorry for me. "And what would you tell them?"

I realized how my story would sound to a normal person. They'd have me locked away in ten seconds flat.

"Listen to me, Frances, because what I'm about to tell you is important. You have something special. A power. A curse. Call it what you want. I knew it the moment I saw you. I can help you use it. Responsibly. Accurately. So it does no harm to you or the people you love."

"What are you talking about?" I said. "This isn't about *me*."

"Let me tell you what happened to Samuel Newman and my part in it. Some of this is going to sound familiar to you," Peter said. He shifted his long legs, and his boots made a rasping sound on the dry wooden floor. "Two days ago, I was taking a late-morning walk along the beach and I began to feel light-headed. This is nothing new to me. It's been happening since I was a boy. I sat down on the stones and I passed out. Some time later, I woke up in a daze and walked back here, to the hut. I began to paint the image you saw on the postcard."

He paused, waiting for me to say that this had happened to me. I didn't give him the pleasure. But I did think of the drawing I had done after my most recent blackout. I had thought that I was just a messed-up kid, and as long as nobody saw the images spilling out of my head, then everything would be fine. Now I was beginning to recalculate my life, and I didn't like the numbers I was getting.

I shook my head. "No," I heard myself say.

"Yes," Peter said, and then continued his story. "I studied the scene with my jeweler's loupe — the little magnifying glass — and began to work on finding the man in the car. The recipient. I had to work fast. The knowledge that's been passed down tells us that we have two days between the drawing and the death. You have to deliver the message in that time, or else . . ." He trailed off, blinked, and then picked up his story from a different place. "Anyway, I knew I had seen his blue Fiesta before, and I was able to trace him from the number plate. He worked in a call center. He was single. He liked dance

music. When you saw me with the loupe yesterday, I was checking the details for the last time."

"Are you seriously telling me . . . ?" I hesitated. It felt like if I said the words, I'd somehow make it true. "Are you trying to tell me that the drawings I do . . . the paintings you do . . . become *real*?"

"Not until the recipient sees the message. Of course, he or she doesn't see the real image the way we do. From what we can work out, they just see a collection of random shapes. Most messengers believe that the image somehow seeps into the subconscious. Nobody really knows how it works. But the recipient has to look at the postcard to make it happen."

I thought for a moment, then gasped. "You made me deliver it to him! You made me . . . You're saying I killed him."

"No," Peter said. "It was his time, that's all. I'm just a messenger. The messages come to me," he said, gesturing at a new postcard that he had on his desk.

I tried to control my breathing. I tried to tell myself this was all lies. Fantastical rubbish. But I was angry about the way he was making me feel. I looked around the room for something to smash. My gaze rested on the postcard. From where I was standing, I couldn't make out exactly what he had painted, but — if I was to believe this man — on that postcard were the details of somebody's death.

Somebody's life.

Peter Kennedy started talking again, but I'd stopped listening. The wind screeched through the gaps in the wooden panels, and I could hear the sea, like a broken telly. There was one inside lock on the door. Peter was mumbling about gifts and prophecies.

I snatched the postcard from the desk, unlocked the door, and sprinted into the noise of the world. Peter got up from his chair and tried to grab me, but I was away.

I ran across the path, nearly knocking over an old bloke with two walking canes, and skipped quickly down the steps in the seawall. It wasn't until I got onto the beach that I began to slow down. I was wearing canvas trainers, and the stones pressed through the soles. The sea had made ridges of pebbles, like dunes, and I tumbled over them. Peter was gaining on me and shouting, but I wasn't listening. There was fear in his voice, a panic I hadn't expected.

The paint on the postcard was tacky on my fingers, but I couldn't bring myself to look at it.

He was closing in. The stones were wet, and I could feel the sea spray on my face, but the sea was going out, being sucked away from me. After what I'd witnessed that day, there was a part of me that truly believed I was saving someone's life. And the part of me that didn't believe it had no problem with the idea of dumping a postcard in the water. But I still had a way to go until I made it to the first waves. I slowed down to look back, and Peter was coming after me. He seemed to glide across the beach stones. I tried to run again, but I tripped. He **tackled me, and** the postcard fell out of my grasp. Peter had me by the ankles, and then the hips. I felt the raw strength of him coming through his hands. My blood thumped.

That end of the beach was pretty much deserted, but I could

see a man walking his dog in the distance. "Help!" I screamed. "I'm being attacked!" The man didn't hear, but it was enough to make Peter release his grip. I stood and retrieved the postcard.

The waves came in, and I staggered toward them. Peter was still on the ground. "Please!" he shouted, and there was such terror in his voice that I turned around to face him.

He got to his knees. "I'm begging you, Frances," he said.

I looked down at the postcard. I was stunned, again, by the photographic perfection of the painting, which showed a man in a suit slumped between two chairs, his eyes rolled back and his hand across his chest. I looked away sharply. "If what you're telling me is true," I said, "then I have to save this man. I can't let what happened this morning happen again. I can't let you deliver this. It's too . . . It's horrible."

"But you don't understand," he said. "If I don't deliver the message, my family will . . . they'll suffer."

I frowned, trying to stay inside his logic, crazy as it seemed. "Well, this man has a family too," I said. "And Samuel Newman had a family. What about *their* lives? Why should I care about your family more than them?"

"It was his time," he said.

That wasn't a good-enough answer. The white sea foam sidled between my feet and sent sparks of cold up my legs. My toes went numb. I turned toward the sea and prepared to drop the postcard.

"I have a son," he said.

I stopped and looked out at the patches of color and steely light on the water.

"A boy," he said. "He's eleven. I'm asking you. Don't do this."

Peter put his hands over his face and watched me from between his fingers, like a frightened kid.

"How can you have an eleven-year-old son? How old *are* you?"

"I was very young when he was born. I was still a teenager."

I tried to take it all in.

"Please," he said. "He's just a child."

He'd got me.

I walked out of the water toward him, and he stood slowly. "Thank you," he said quietly. "I'm sorry I made you deliver the card to Samuel Newman. I handled it badly. But I just wanted you to understand the power you have."

I shook my head. "You're wrong about me," I said.

"I'm not. You've had the blackouts. You've made the images. It's true, isn't it?"

"It's not the same," I said.

"You're young and your gift hasn't developed yet," he said. He was trembling slightly. "I've been through what you're going through. Mostly, you'll have produced duds. Just unfinished scribbles. Your powers are growing, though. It won't be long. That's why you came to me."

"I didn't come to you!"

"I can help you control it. Help keep your family safe. The people you love."

"I'm not like you," I said, my anger about what I'd been through that day suddenly coming back. "Look at you. You're a mess."

He was trembling, almost in tears. "Well, can't you imagine why?" he said.

"I'm not going to end up like you."

"There's no choice. I don't know why this happens to us, but it does. You mustn't feel guilty."

He held out his hand for the postcard, and I gave it to him. "Keep your postcard, and keep the hell away from me," I said.

And I left him there, staring out to sea.

SIX

I went to the arcades on the pier that afternoon. I reckon I needed the red and yellow flashing lights and the people around me. I needed silly childish noises. Whizbangs and whistles, and the jingle of coins. I was properly shaken up. At one point, I looked over at a driving game, and I swear I saw the man from that morning, his head on the steering wheel, his neck badly cocked. But it was just a vision. Just another sign I was losing it.

I went out for some fresh air. The wind caused the little plastic windmills outside the toy shop to whir. In spite of the muggy summer weather, a few kids were tombstoning off the pier, their shouts cut off each time by the water. I thought of that postcard, the man with his hand on his heart. Could it be true that the man would now die? I wondered how many people Peter Kennedy had painted. Who would be next? Perhaps one of the kids jumping off the pier. Maybe it would be the woman who operated the teacup ride or the man who was skateboarding down the sea path, using two golf umbrellas as sails.

As if that thought weren't bad enough, I had to consider the possibility that I had done something similar. I thought about the scene from my most recent drawing. Peter had said my abilities were growing. Was this what the blackouts meant? Was I going to become a monster? A killer? I'd have to spend my days hiding out, like Peter Kennedy.

Don't get me wrong, I was a rational person, and it was hard to believe what Peter had told me, especially as he seemed so unsure about the details. But how else could he have known about my blackouts? And I'd seen what I'd seen on Landsmere Road that morning.

Soon, the sky began to darken and the lights of the rides bloomed in the gray. I walked back toward Auntie Lizzie's. What worried me most was this: Peter had said that if he didn't deliver his messages, his family would suffer. Until this week, my drawings had just been weird harmless-looking sketches — a face here, a scribble there. But the last drawing I'd done was different. I thought of it now, sitting at the bottom of my bag. Two days. That meant, by his logic, I had until tomorrow morning.

Auntie Lizzie and Uncle Robert were lying on the plush white sofas watching TV. "There's a tuna salad in the fridge, Fran," Auntie Lizzie said through a yawn, and I nodded. Uncle Robert smiled openly at me, but I turned away, not wanting him to see how I was feeling. I needed to keep the details of the day to myself.

"Any calls, Auntie Lizzie?" I said.

"No, sorry, love," she said.

I went upstairs to check on Max. His door was ajar. "Maxi," I said. No answer. I walked in. He was sitting cross-legged on his bed with his eyes closed, his glasses on the bedside table. Black baggy track pants and a black T-shirt. He was totally still.

"Max," I said.

He opened one eye and breathed softly. It took him another few moments to wake fully. "Hi, Frances," he said.

"What the bloody hell are you doing?" I said. "Are you doing yoga? I thought you were — you know — a *boy*?"

He smiled. "It's not yoga. I was meditating. They teach us at kendo."

"Where's that?" I said.

"It's not a place — it's a discipline. It's sort of like sword fighting, except with wooden sticks."

"Oh, the one with the fencing masks," I said.

"Well . . . yes, OK."

I sat on his bed and tried on his spectacles. The world was a total blur. I hadn't realized how bad his eyes were. "God, Maxi, these are making me feel sick," I said. He took the glasses from me and put them on.

"Did you have a good afternoon?" he said.

"No. Did you?"

"It was fine. I feel pretty good. Balanced."

"Right, right." I thought maybe he was stoned. "You not going out with your mates?"

"No. I got a text from them this afternoon. They were in La Senza."

"The bra shop?" I said. "What were they doing in there?"

"Looking," Max said.

"Jesus. What a bunch of freaks," I said, although Peter Kennedy had taken my definition of the word "freak" to a whole new level recently. "If that's what they get up to, it's no wonder you stay home with your eyes closed."

He smiled again. "In kendo, you have to learn to control the mind. To get to a point of stillness where you can see what your opponent is going to do next — where you can see what you are going to do next, and then change it."

"Like seeing the future," I said sadly.

"Kind of. Like *controlling* the future."

"So what's in the crystal ball, Maxi? What's in store for me? Any ideas? Will I get to snog Todd Garner from year twelve?"

Max took a deep breath and pretended to look into the future. "I'm seeing . . . yes . . . he'll try to feel you up, and you'll slap him."

I laughed. "I probably wouldn't slap him."

"To be honest," he said, "it takes ages to learn kendo. I've got a long way to go. Most of the people who make *hachi-dan,* the highest rank, are in their sixties and seventies. Lightning fast."

"I'd better spend the next fifty-odd years kicking your arse then, hadn't I? Before you get good."

"You should see them on the videos. It's amazing."

"Really? Isn't it funny, watching all those old blokes sword fighting?"

"They're wearing masks and robes. You can't tell how old they are. I'm saving up for the gear. It's pretty expensive, and Dad won't pay."

I thought of Johnny boxing. He had told me once that after a certain number of years of being punched every day, boxers get what's known as a "conditioned face." The skin becomes so tough that they don't get cuts anymore. Johnny thought that was a good thing, but I didn't. I looked at my cousin, with his delicate cheekbones. "If you have to do a martial art, Maxi, I'm glad you'll be wearing pads and a mask."

I went back to my room and lay down. I took one of my beloved Berol Venus pencils out of the tin and looked down the length of it. The bright-green cracks in the dark-green varnish now looked like some kind of poison ready to leak out. I sniffed up the spicy scent of the wood and graphite, which reminded me of home.

There was a part of me that wished my brother would hand himself in, just so I could see him again. I knew that was selfish. I had to hope he was safe. Then I thought about Peter Kennedy and the picture under my bed. Maybe, if I didn't deliver my "message," I would put Johnny in danger.

I tried to think of positive things, to calm myself down and take my mind off the day I'd had. Johnny used to pick me up from junior school. I was always so proud to see him out the classroom window — the ragbag rebel in his vest and jeans, with a couple of ice pops. As time went on, he wore his *Top Gun* aviator sunglasses all the time — usually to hide his black or bloodied eyes. I could hear him flirting with the mothers at the gates, always in that jokey polite tone of his. *"Afternoon, Mrs. H. That's a very fetching blouse you've got on."* They loved it.

We'd walk home together, and he'd sit on the end of my

bed and tell me stories about our dad. I would look at Johnny and see myself reflected twice in his shades. Then we'd watch *Home and Away*.

According to Johnny, our dad had walked across America holding two bricks by his fingers, and — although it wasn't in the *Guinness Book of World Records* because of an error — that was one of the most grueling tests a man could endure. "Once, before you were born," Johnny said, "we were riding through the countryside in the Citroën, and Mum said to Dad, 'What's for dinner?' and Dad said, 'Lamb.' He jumped out of the car, hopped over a fence, picked up a sheep from this field, and stuffed it in the trunk."

When he wore his parka, my dad could make it look as though his head had turned 360 degrees. He could recall the names of all the kings and queens of England, and every capital city in the world. "He was smart, you see. That's where you get it from," Johnny would say. "I got the brick-carrying gene."

I spent a good deal of my childhood with this image of my dad as a charming, record-breaking scamp. A man who leaped over fences and stored history. A master of optical illusions. Maybe after the head-turning trick, I thought, he'd just made himself disappear. But I could see the love in Johnny's eyes when he told the stories.

That night, I fell asleep in Auntie Lizzie's house, imagining Johnny's weight on the end of my bed, like in the old days. But in my dreams, I felt Peter Kennedy's big hands on my hips and ankles, the way he'd grabbed me on the beach. In my dreams, I couldn't figure out if I was scared or excited.

* * *

I woke a few hours later to the sound of quick, heavy footsteps on the landing. I half expected Peter Kennedy to smash through my door. I poked my head out and saw the toilet light on across the landing. Auntie Lizzie, in her nightdress, was holding on to Max, who was bent over the bath, puking.

"Robert!" she shouted.

Uncle Robert came out onto the landing in his boxer shorts and a faded T-shirt, his hair genuinely a mess. "Max! What's going on?" he said. "Have you been drinking?"

"He's been in the house all night, Robert," Auntie Lizzie said.

"Is everything OK?" I asked.

Auntie Lizzie turned around, and her expression showed me that it wasn't. "It's fine, Frances, yes. It'll be fine. A spot of food poisoning, probably."

She turned back to Max, and I caught a glimpse of his face. His eyes were rolling back in his head. He was sick again.

"Oh, God, Robert," Auntie Lizzie said. "He's bringing up blood."

"It's his stomach lining," Uncle Robert said. His voice had softened up. He was worried. "Should we call someone, Liz?"

I backed away into the bedroom, took out my kit bag and retrieved the crumpled drawing. I looked at the image of a cat, its neck clamped between the jaws of a dog. I thought back to what Peter Kennedy had said. Surely he couldn't be right. Could it be *me* doing this? Was I killing Max by not delivering the message? Listening to Max struggling for breath, it was suddenly possible to believe him. There wasn't much of a decision to make. I slipped on my shoes — still wet from the sea — and went downstairs with the picture.

When I opened the big steel fridge, the light and the cold flooded the kitchen. The tuna salad was still in there, under tin foil. I took it out and made my way quickly through the house and into the cool street.

The pavement still held a little of the day's heat, and the streetlights looked like honey and lemon Lockets. I wandered around and sucked my lips to make that noise that pet people make. I'd left the front door open, and I could hear Uncle Robert talking on the phone, outright panic in his voice now. *He must be calling the ambulance*, I thought.

"Here, kitty," I said. I took the foil off the salad and picked out the flakes of tuna, crumbled them between my fingers. "Here, kitty, kitty. Come on. Please, come on."

I was shaking now. I suddenly had a vision of Max as a little boy, his big shaggy hair. "Come on, you stupid cat!" I shouted into the street.

The cat came out from between two cars, meowing, its mouth so wide I could see its pink tongue. I shook some tuna off my hand onto the pavement, and the cat licked it up. I put out my fingers, and it chewed at the little gray bits of fish. Its teeth were like hot needles, but I didn't mind.

"There you go, puss," I said.

I smoothed out the drawing on my thigh and saw the scene for the last time.

A workman in a cap.

A scruffy-looking man in his thirties.

An old woman behind a half-open door, terrified.

A dog, a cat.

"I'm very sorry, but this has got to be done," I said as I showed the drawing to the cat. I was struck suddenly by how mad this was. As if *this* could kill anything. As if *I* could save Max. The cat lifted one front leg and pawed at the picture, but then got back to the important business of eating its surprise fish supper. I held the picture out until my arm got tired, and I felt a sort of calm come over me. The street was so peaceful. Just the swish of leaves and the hiss of cars from the main road. Somehow I knew it had worked.

The doomed cat walked past me, pressing its body against my shin, like they do. I stood up in time to see Robert stomping out into the front garden in his flip-flops, his mobile phone pressed to his ear. "I called eight minutes ago," he was saying. "We're a four-minute drive from the hospital. . . . What? Yes, I understand that, but this is terrible. Our boy is . . . Yes. I know you are. I'm sorry. Two minutes, OK. Thank you."

He ended the call and put his head in his hands. Then he saw me. "Frances. What are you doing? Are you . . . ? You're feeding a cat. Frances, Max is very sick. I hardly think this is the time to . . ."

I smiled at him and walked over. "He's gonna be all right, Uncle Robert. It's gonna be fine. I promise."

He looked at me in a sort of dumb shock. It was like all of the fight had gone out of him, and he had accepted that he had no control over the world. *He* didn't. I put my hand on his arm because I felt sorry for him, and then I walked back into the house and up the stairs. I didn't rush. With every moment that passed, I became more certain that there was no longer any cause for alarm. Sure enough, when I got to the landing, Max was slumped against the bath with a sopping facecloth on his forehead, and Auntie Lizzie was running her fingers through his wet hair. It looked like he was meditating. Perfectly well, perfectly at peace.

I went to bed, shuddering. The ambulance arrived, then left. I lay there, exhausted and sleepless.

SEVEN

In the morning, I sneaked into Max's room and sat on his bed. If you looked hard enough, you could see the clues to the little boy he used to be: the windup false teeth on his bedside table, the corner of a wall chart identifying different kinds of beetles sticking out from under his Death Cab for Cutie poster, a box in the corner full of toys. A radio-controlled car with Han Solo sprawled across the bonnet.

"Maxi," I whispered.

He stirred from his sleep and licked his lips. It was early. "What is it?" he said, squinting.

"I just wanted to make sure you were OK," I said.

"Uh-huh."

"Are you sure?"

"I feel . . ." He yawned. "I feel incredible," he said.

I smiled and pinched his cheek. "Good. Listen, Karate Kid, will you teach me how to do that mind-control thing sometime?"

"It takes many years to understand the ways of—"

"Knock it off! I'm a fast learner, Maxwell. You'd be surprised."

"OK, young apprentice," he said in the voice of a slow-talking mentor. "I will school you in the ways of the kendo masters. But first, I must sleep."

I pulled the duvet down over his toes, went back to my room, and sat by the window.

I didn't want to watch what was about to unfold, but I told myself that I had to. I needed to know if any of this was real. As time drifted by, I became more and more certain that Peter Kennedy's ideas were crazy and that Max throwing up was just a weird coincidence.

The street was fairly quiet but for the wind. Helmstown was at the mercy of the weather, and so far it had been a rubbish summer. There was a van parked at the end of the road, and a workman in a big baseball cap got out, coughing. I couldn't see the cat anywhere, but I could feel its presence behind the parked cars.

I recognized the crusty guy who came round the corner from my drawing. His dog waddled just behind him. I took a deep breath. The guy was on his mobile, and I could hear him through the window. "For Jesus' sake, Mum, it's fifty quid. You're not gonna miss it. . . . " Suddenly I hated him.

The dog got a move on and galloped away from its owner. I didn't turn my head to watch.

My heart was hammering now. I heard the dog barking and the cat hissing. Then the cat screeched once and its voice was taken. Still I didn't look. Instead, I watched the face of the workman change to horror as he looked over at the developing scene. He began to run toward the noise.

"Milo, no!" the crusty guy shouted. "No! Get off him!"

I heard a front door open, and the old woman came out. I didn't need to look at her, because I'd seen her in the picture. I'd seen her broken features. "Stop! Stop him! It's killing my cat! My baby! Oh, God!"

I heard the door slam and then open again. The old woman was too frail to take on the dog. She could barely watch, but she couldn't look away.

I heard the growl of the dog.

I heard the workman shouting.

The pathetic voice of the crusty guy. "Milo, no! Oh, Jesus! I'm sorry! I'm so sorry!"

I heard the workman's hand slapping the dog's hide.

The woman still screaming.

I knew without looking: my picture was complete.

"Let go!" the workman said. "Come on, boy. I mean it."

The cat landed softly. I heard the gentle thud. There was no mistaking it. The old woman moaned. The crusty guy apologized and then kicked his dog.

"Watch it, you!" the workman said. "People like you shouldn't be allowed to keep dogs. I saw it happen, so if she wants to report you, I'm a witness."

But I was the real witness. The witness and the killer. I had seen it all long before anyone else had. I had made it happen.

* * *

My plan for the rest of the day was this: to stay in my room and not kill anything. That afternoon, Auntie Lizzie gave up trying to coax me downstairs and came in. She sat at the end of the bed with a small envelope.

"Any news about Johnny?" I asked.

"No. I called your mum today and she said —"

"She picked up the phone for you?"

"Well . . . yes . . . but only because . . . I suppose I just called at the right time of day."

"Yeah, sure," I said.

"She probably wants to keep you out of it."

"I don't want to be *kept out of it*. What did she say? Has Johnny been in touch?"

"No," Lizzie said. She opened her mouth to speak again but didn't. We were quiet for a moment.

"Mum doesn't think he's coming back, does she?" I said.

"You know what she's like. She hardly ever looks on the bright side."

"You don't seem very optimistic yourself, Auntie Lizzie."

She sighed and took some photos out of the envelope. "I thought these photographs might cheer you up," she said.

Johnny dressed as a Teenage Mutant Ninja Turtle carrying little old me in his green arms; Mum wearing boxing gloves, pretending to fight little Johnny, who was standing on the sofa at Nana's house in Whiteslade; Mum, me, and Nana in our cozzies on the beach, pouting like beauty queens. There were a couple taken inside the little shed near Nana's house that Johnny used as a gym, and I laughed at the one of me hanging off Johnny's bicep, all the press cuttings and boxing quotes stuck to the wall behind us. There was another little sign hung on the wall, too, and Lizzie put on her glasses to read it. "God Bless This Mess."

"God bless it," I said, staring at Johnny and me in the shed. "Can I keep this one?"

"It's yours," Auntie Lizzie said. She kissed me on the head and left the room.

That's when I started to feel the weariness again. It's the first sign. Your limbs go heavy. I got up from the bed and opened the window, but the fresh air didn't pep me up much. Then I started to smell smoke, just as I had done before. It smells like the aftermath of a firework. I tried to shout. I wasn't calling for help. I was just angry and afraid.

I managed to get to the bed before my sight started to go.

When I fully surfaced, I was on the floor, with my sketch pad open. An hour had passed. The drawing was sharper this time, and more disturbing. "Please, God," I said quietly. In the picture, there was an old man lying still at the bottom of a bath, his mouth open, his perfect teeth bared, his lips dark, the water covering his open eyes. It was difficult to believe something so complicated had come from my own hands. The other sketches in my pad were pitiful in comparison. It was the best, and worst, thing I'd ever done. I threw it across the room and backed away as if the sketch pad were some poisonous creature.

I knew that I needed help, and I knew there was only one person I could go to. Whether I wanted to or not.

EIGHT

The next day, I found him standing on the path outside his beach hut with a bunch of postcards. A group of women swarmed around him. They all wore white jackets with KELLY'S HEN written on the back in pink. They wore denim skirts and cowboy boots, and most of them had cowboy hats on strings around their necks. The goose bumps stood out on their fake-tanned legs.

I took a long route round and hid behind Peter's hut for a moment, watching. He was talking to Kelly, who was obviously the one getting married.

"You just here for the weekend?" Peter said.

"No, we're doing a whole week," Kelly said. "My last proper week with the girls. Thought we'd come to the seaside."

"Great," Peter said. "Oh, look. These are the more naughty postcards."

He flicked through the pile of cards in his hands. I was close enough to see them. Kelly threw her head back and laughed. "Look at that one! Here, Treez, this guy looks like your Gav!"

She showed the postcard to another woman, who cackled and said, "Yeah, chance would be a fine thing."

Peter and Kelly went through a few more postcards together. Most of them were photos of male strippers or breasts with faces painted on them. But one of them wasn't. One of them was a painting of a street, with an ambulance and a woman lying on a stretcher.

"This one's a bit weird," Kelly said. "Have you got any of Prince Harry?"

Peter held the postcard in front of her for a moment before putting it to the bottom of the pile. I knew what it was. It was a message. I jumped from behind the hut and smashed the postcards out of his hand.

"Oi! Steady on, girl!" said Kelly. "What's your problem?"

I ignored her and turned to Peter. He shook his head. "It's too late," he said in a low voice. "She's seen it."

I looked at all the cards scattering along the path. I couldn't see which one was the message. It had blended into the mass, and before I had a chance to respond, a seagull swooped down and sent a big white dollop toward the crowd of women. It spattered on the ground. Kelly jumped back.

"It's good luck when a seagull poos on you, Kel," one of the women said.

Kelly looked herself over. "I think he missed," she said. "Hey, let's go for a paddle!"

They picked up a few of the postcards, returned them to Peter, and then clopped over to the steps leading down to the beach.

I turned to Peter, who was putting as many of his postcards as he could back into the rack. Some of them blew down the path. "When did you draw that one?"

"Early hours of this morning," he said.

"Don't you feel bad?" I said.

"I don't know anymore," he said. "It's like when you swim in the sea in January. For a while, you don't think you can bear it, but eventually you just go numb."

I shook my head and thought of the cat screeching this morning, the sketch of the dead old man in my rucksack.

"Come on," he said. "I'll buy you a coffee."

He walked off down the path, his shoulders hunched, his painting hand in his pocket. I followed.

"That woman," I said. "When she saw the painting, she didn't even flinch."

He sighed. "I told you before. It seems that most people only see a surface image of random shapes. The sort of things that cubist artists used to paint. Tabby, my mentor, thought that the average person's brain isn't built in a way that can consciously register a death scene. They can't decode it with their eyes. It's too much for them. *You* can see the death scenes perfectly, though, can't you? You don't need any more proof that you're a messenger."

"I killed a cat," I said sadly.

He shook his head. "You just delivered the message. Was it a cat you knew?"

"We weren't close," I said.

He smiled.

"There's more, though. I drew a person."

He nodded. "Let's not talk about it here," he said.

We joined the back of the queue for the Coffee Shack. The dark-haired bloke in front of us was in his early twenties and had a gray whippet. I'd seen him before. I stroked the whippet's muzzle for a while. Since coming to Helmstown, I'd watched the man come out of his house on plenty of occasions, and it occurred to me that he lived two doors down from a really nice coffeehouse, yet he had come all the way down here for a plastic cup of Nescafé. It wasn't long before I realized why.

The woman behind the counter was about the same age, and she had long red hair and a nice figure. Her name badge said HELEN. She smiled at the whippet as the guy went up to order. "Hello, boy," she said.

"Hello," the dark-haired man replied before he realized she was talking to his dog. I watched the back of his neck turn red.

I whispered to Peter, "I think the whippet guy fancies Helen."

Peter shrugged. "It'd be nice if he could fancy her when I wasn't behind him in the queue."

I rolled my eyes. "You're not a romantic, then?" I said. "What about the mother of your son?"

"I don't want to talk about it," he said.

"But—"

"Trust me. When you're a messenger, relationships don't work out. The closer you get to someone, the harder it becomes." Then something occurred to him. "You don't have a boyfriend, do you?"

"No," I said. "I'm waiting for the right man."

He sniffed at that.

"What?" I said.

"The right man," he said. "People always confuse love with destiny. When people fall in love, they say that everything in their life has been leading to that moment. But every moment in your life leads to death, not love. Death. Every twist, every turn. Every decision, good or bad."

"God, that's a lovely way of looking at it," I said.

"I'm just telling you the facts. Death is waiting for all of us. Your death day is out there, just like your birthday. It's unstoppable. The disease that kills you might be there already, the bad cells might be lurking in your organs."

"Lurking in my organs?" I said sarcastically.

He pointed at a woman on the sea path, who was shouting at a toddler. "Maybe that little boy will grow up to kill me. Maybe his abusive mother is right now doing the damage that will drive him to drink."

"A boozing baby?"

"I'm talking about the future. Perhaps in twenty years, he'll get drunk, get in his car, and run me over. And everything that happens to me and him between now and then — everything we do — is just a way of getting us to that place and time."

The man with the whippet trundled off with his drink, and Peter stepped up to the counter. There was a confidence in his movements that the boys I knew back home didn't have. Those boys were all so well groomed, almost girlish in their care over their appearance, and here was this man, his shoulders muscled up, who didn't give a damn about the whitish dust all over his tracksuit top. I found that really hot. And yet he was telling me that even buying a cup of tea was just one more step along the road to the cemetery. It was depressing.

"So you're saying death is more important than love?" I said as Helen busied herself with the Styrofoam cups.

"Of course it is."

I sighed, deeply. "Christ, don't you know any jokes?"

To be fair, he laughed at that. We both laughed. But then I saw the newspaper lying on an empty table. LOCAL POLITICIAN DIES AT GALA DINNER. A brief look at the photograph told me it was the man whose death scene I had held above the waves two days earlier.

"It's unstoppable," Peter said quietly.

We took the drinks back to his hut. Inside, out of the wind, Peter unzipped his top very slightly, and I noticed that he wasn't wearing a T-shirt underneath. I could see the hollow at his throat, that one vulnerable point, and the sinews of his chest. I couldn't look away. He caught me staring, and I panicked. "You'll catch your death, dressed like that," I blurted out, trying to cover myself.

"It's July," he said, and I blushed.

I studied the paintings on the wall, which — thankfully — contained no cubist art and no scenes of death. They were paintings of the sea. Sometimes there were boats; sometimes he'd painted cliffs or little coastal villages. They didn't have the hyper-real feeling of his messages, but they were nice.

"You sometimes paint for pleasure, then?" I said.

"I used to. Used to sell a few, too. Not so much, these days. Don't have the time."

"What's your day job?"

"I'm a part-time plasterer." Which explained the dust.

"Not quite as artistic, is it?"

"I like it because it's boring."

"Not many part-time plasterers can afford a Helmstown beach hut," I said.

"I inherited some money when my father died."

In one of the paintings, the sea and sky were nearly the same metallic gray, and I almost didn't notice the small white-sailed boat in the corner of the scene. "It's ace, this one," I said. "I like the way the boat is off to the side, like it's not the point."

"Thank you," he said.

We both knew I had questions about what was happening to me, but we needed this moment of calm first. He sat on his chair, and I sat on the floor.

"You know, I don't have all the answers," he said eventually. "Nobody does."

"You've got more answers than me," I said.

He shrugged. "What do you want to know?"

"Nothing. Everything," I said.

"I can only tell you what Tabby told me and what I've observed. I'm just a cog in the machine." He looked at his boots, as if he was uncomfortable talking about these things, as if he thought it was unlucky to discuss them.

"What happens if I miss the deadline?" I said.

"From what we know . . . someone close to you dies instead. A life for a life."

"That's . . . I don't understand."

"Death must be satisfied, I guess. The scales have to be balanced."

"*How* do you know it's true?"

He closed his eyes and shook his head slowly.

"Jesus. Did you ever miss one?" I said.

"Look. Death is not the kind of thing you can be sure about. It's a force of nature. People have been studying it for thousands of years, and they know nothing. It's bigger than us. All I can do is trust the knowledge that's out there and try to pass it on to you. I believed Tabby. I trusted her. The things she said made *sense* to me, and I've seen proof that she was right about lots of them. I've learned from experience, too. In my opinion, there is a simple set of rules, and you should learn them rather than asking any big questions. You make the message. You find the recipient. You show them the message. Or you face the consequences."

I shook my head. "Where's your family? Where's your son?"

The ropes of muscle in his chest tightened. "Next question," he said.

"How many messengers are there?"

"Who knows? Two? Two million? I've only met Tabby and you, but I'm pretty sure I've recognized others."

"And you didn't speak to them! Why not?"

"Once you know what a messenger does, why the hell would you want to meet one?"

"You wanted to meet me, didn't you?"

He didn't answer that. He rubbed his face and turned to his desk. I could see that he was becoming agitated, but I wasn't going to give up. I needed information.

"How do you get round to all the people that have to die?" I said. "Thousands of people die every day. Are they all killed by messengers? Do some just die anyway?"

"I don't hold the mysteries of the universe! You expect me to know things because I'm a messenger, but being a messenger brings home how little I know. How little you can *do*, as a human," he said. "I hate these questions."

"Don't you think they're important? I mean, don't you want to know where you fit in? What your place in the world is?" I asked.

"Why?" He turned back to me.

"*Why?* Well, otherwise, you don't know what you're doing with your life."

"Who does? Everyone thinks they're the center of the universe, but really we're just tiny insignificant specks. We're part of something we'll never understand, and maybe it's better that way."

Insignificant speck, I thought. *Charming.*

"So who was this Tabby, then?" I said, trying to get back to specifics.

"Tabby Smith. She did abstract watercolors. Every messenger has their medium, I suppose. She was so intelligent.

She had studied hard under her own mentor and learned everything she could. She taught me all I know about being a messenger."

"How did you meet?"

"She lived in a tower block back home. I just found myself spending time there. I didn't know why."

Those words hung in the air between us. I suppose we were thinking of our own first meeting. He continued. "I guess I knew something was wrong with me, and I had this feeling she could help. She did. I would have done anything for her. She taught me how to control my gift."

"But you *don't* control it," I said, thinking of Kelly the Hen having her last paddle in the sea.

"I live with it."

"The people you paint don't."

He stood, but there was really nowhere to go in his beach hut. It was too small to pace up and down, so he just put his hands on his hips and sighed.

"When I was about your age," he said, "Tabby Smith told me I might one day want to leave my family and move away. She'd done so herself. Her theory was that messengers draw or paint those people who pass through their minds. It might be someone you glimpsed for a second through the window of a café. It might be your mother. My father had already died — I never painted him, thank God — and although my family wasn't particularly loving, I didn't want to kill them. So I came south with my inheritance money and became a plasterer's apprentice in Hartsleigh, not far from here."

"Where's Tabby Smith now?" I said.

"She's dead," he said. His eyes were watering, but it could have been the sea air rushing through the gap beneath the door. "She died just before I moved from the north."

"I'm sorry," I said.

He shook his head.

"Why do we think these violent thoughts, Peter?" I said. "Why are they in our minds?"

"I suppose they're in everyone's minds. Everyone has violent thoughts," he said. "Not much you can do about it."

"Haven't you tried controlling them? Isn't there any way? I mean, you can control your thoughts when you don't want to laugh or cry. So can't we stop the visions or change them?"

"I doubt it," he said. "Tabby said that kind of thing could be dangerous."

I was getting fed up now. We were in a desperate situation. We needed to find a way out of it, and he wasn't helping. "Why are you being like this?" I said. "Why are you being so negative?"

"What are you talking about?" he said.

I paused. "You get a kick out of being a messenger, don't you?" I was trying to wind him up, to get a rise out of him.

"No," he said.

"Yes, you do. I saw you with that woman going through the postcards. You were having the time of your life."

"I was not. This is something we have to . . . Tabby said that death is a necessary force. Without it, the world would fall apart. I believe that. Think of the consequences!"

"Imagine how her fella's going to feel. Eh? He's gearing up for the wedding. And you could see how excited *she* was. You're going to take all that away from her without even trying to stop it. You're going to rob the fiancé of the woman he loves. Imagine how that feels."

"You don't know anything about me!" he said. "Or what I've been through. You can't just come in here and judge me. That woman is going to drink herself into a coma. She's a drunk."

"Now who's judging?"

He took a pace toward me, and I stood up, backed away. I could see the pads of muscle in his hands. I was scared, of course, but there was a flicker of electricity that went through me too.

"Listen," he said, unclenching his fists. "I'm trying to help. I can help you manage what's happening to you. But if you keep pushing me like this, I'll walk away and leave you to make a mess of your life."

"Well, I reckon you'd know something about that," I said.

"Get out," he said, opening the door.

"You listen to me, *Pete*," I said. "When I've got a problem, I go out and try things. I try to solve it. I don't waste away in a bloody hut going, '*Woe is me — everything's inevitable.*' Now maybe you're right — maybe I do have this messed-up curse or whatever. But it's *my* messed-up curse, and I can choose what to do with it. You can carry on just drawing the future, if you like. But I'm going to *change* it."

He made another move toward me, and I nearly tripped over, backing out the door. "Great," he said sarcastically. "I'm glad you know so much about all of this. I'm glad you're so powerful. Good luck with your newfound talent. And good bloody riddance."

He slammed the door, and I suddenly found myself outside, with the peaceful noises of the sea and the gulls and jangling boat masts.

"Prick!" I shouted at the door.

It opened, and I ran until I could barely breathe. I bent over and rested at the side of the path, looking back to check that Peter wasn't following. Something caught my eye in the grass verge. A scattering of four or five postcards. And there it was among them: the message. I picked the postcard up and looked closely. I could just about make out Kelly the Hen lying on a stretcher on a busy street, paramedics surrounding her, a cowboy hat on the ground. I made my calculations. Two days. It was due to happen on Friday night. I put the postcard in my pocket.

NINE

Max tried to teach me some of his mind- control skills. I met him down by the "Women-Only Disco" on the beach. The gray summer continued, and that afternoon was windy and cold. I kept a close eye on Max: I was worried that I still hadn't made any attempt to find the old man in the sketch I'd drawn, and I didn't want poor old Maxi to start chucking up again. But part of me was still in denial, unable to believe any of it.

We bought cockles from a stall, soaked them in salt and vinegar, picked them out with cocktail sticks, and washed them down with Diet Coke, our mouths all gritty and sweet and sour.

"You're definitely feeling better, then?" I said.

"Yeah. Much better, thanks."

"What's the point of a women-only disco?" I said. "Is that a Helmstown thing?"

"I don't know. A friend of mine, Jake, says he came down here one night and looked through the window, and all the women were semi-naked and making out and stuff."

"Sounds like this Jake is a liar," I said.

"He definitely needs therapy," Max said seriously, polishing his glasses.

"So are we going to do some meditating?" I said.

"Sure — why not? Let's go onto the beach. The waves are, you know, soothing."

There was nobody up that end of the beach. It smelled of fish and rubbish, and the sea was foamy and brown, like Coke sloshing round in a bottle. We sat on the stones, and Max tried to show me the lotus position, but it was tough because we were both in skinny jeans.

"Close your eyes," said Max.

I did. Immediately, the sea appeared in my mind. It became like a massive building, towering over us.

"First you need to tense each part of your body," Max said, shouting above the noise of the waves. "Start with your neck. Really tense it up. Then let it go. It should feel warm. A little tingly."

It felt freezing cold.

"Move on to your shoulders. Make sure you're aware of your breathing. Try to breathe into the pit of your stomach. It's all about becoming aware of your body."

"It's quite funny that this is supposed to be relaxing, but we're having to shout," I said.

"What?" Max said. I opened one eye, but he was smiling.

We went through the various parts of the body, tensing and relaxing. "It's pretty cold out here, Maxi," I said.

"Yes. Feel it; become aware of it."

"I'm very bloody aware of it."

"Acknowledge it and control it. That's the aim. Feel your warm blood going to the cold parts and circulating."

I tried to do that for a while. "Maxi," I said.

"Yes."

"My bum's gone to sleep."

"Right. You don't want it to go to sleep. You want it to relax, but not sleep."

I smiled. Despite everything that had happened that day, I started to feel calm. The sea slid off the pebbles. Max had told me to empty my mind. To acknowledge each thought and just let it go.

The cat. Let it go.

Peter Kennedy. His strong chest and narrow soulful eyes. Let it go.

My anger at Peter Kennedy and his resigned, inactive ways. Gone.

The thought of my next blackout. Gone.

Johnny . . . well, it was harder to let go of Johnny. Of the memories. I couldn't stop these.

Memory One: Johnny was on the end of my bed in his aviators, telling me the story of how he'd once been dismantling a ballpoint pen. He'd slipped off his chair, and the spring had slid into his thumb, right down under the nail. He was only little, and he'd screamed in pain. Mum and Granddad and Nana had tried to yank it out, but it was stuck deep in his flesh. All the tugging had made it hurt even worse. Then Dad came along, and he very gently twisted it four or five times, and it wound out just as it had gone in.

"You see," Johnny had said to me. "He was always using his head."

Even at the time I had thought that twisting out the spring was a pretty obvious solution, but I never said anything.

Memory Two: The days before Johnny's first fight following the Helmstown defeat. Granddad was round again, and the house had returned to that regime of early-morning running and chewing bubble gum. One afternoon, I found Johnny taking a nap on the old sofa, with its loose-stitch pattern of peacocks and trees. His mouth was open and he was drooling. His hand was on the arm of the sofa, the fingers spread. I was only six, but I'd be damned if I was going to let him get into a boxing ring and get pummeled again. So I went to the cupboard and got a hammer out of the tool kit my dad had left behind. I went back to the living room and whispered, "Dear Johnny, I am sorry, but it's for your own good." And I took aim and brought down that hammer on his hand with every bit of strength I had.

He jumped up like a squirrel, screaming, "Dad, no! Please!"

My hammer blow had obviously gone into his dreams.

When he saw me, his eyes widened. He looked at his hand, then back at me. He started laughing. His eyes were streaming, and he was shouting, "Ouch. Jesus!" But he was laughing his head off.

It was a heavy hammer, and I broke his middle finger. They strapped it up, he fought, and he lost.

Memory Three: I had not thought about this for a long time. After the Helmstown fight, I'd woken from my blackout back at Nana's house in Whiteslade. I was distressed to see Johnny standing above me. I didn't recognize him. He wasn't wearing his sunglasses, and one of his eyes was swollen shut. His nostrils were stuffed with cotton wool, and his lip looked like some kind of sea creature. He'd washed his hair, which had gone fluffy and looked weird against his shiny skin. "God, Johnny," I whispered.

"You see? I'm OK," he said. "There's nothing wrong with me."

I did see, and there was plenty wrong with him.

I screamed and jumped out of bed. I ran through the house. I picked up my colored pencils and some paper, and I scarpered outside, sprinting through the garden in my socks, over the stone wall, through the field, toward the shed — that old disused shed on the hill. I started to feel sick. It wasn't like I was being chased. It was like I was running *toward* something, something absolutely terrifying. And I couldn't stop.

I snapped out of the trance when the sea foam reached my knees. I stood up, sharpish. "Max?"

"Tide's coming in," he said. He was behind me. "Shall we go home? You look shattered."

I smiled weakly, wondering why my thoughts kept flashing

back to that day at Nana's. "I'm fine," I said. I looked up above the seawall, at the beach huts and the paths. "Yes. Let's go home. But can we walk the long way round?"

We passed through town at twilight, and the place was coming to life. The smell of aftershave and lip balm and cheap wine, and kids sitting in the market square and the city garden, drinking shiftily. But they weren't *my* friends. I should have been back home, getting ready to go out with Keisha. Instead, I was stuck here, trying to think of ways to stop an old man and a young woman called Kelly from dying.

"Maxi?"

"Yes."

"We're all going to die, right?"

"Well, that's lightened the mood, Frances."

"No, I'm serious. I'm being philosophical. I mean, it's only a matter of time before we go. The clock is ticking for all of us."

"Yes, but death isn't a time," Max said. "It's a *place,* really."

That made sense to me, of course. Peter was painting scenes. He was painting places. "If you could see the scene of your death in advance, what would you do?" I asked.

"God, you're so *emo* these days."

"Come on, Maxi, humor me."

"If I knew where I was going to die, I would go to that place beforehand and remove anything hazardous," he said, and laughed.

"You what?" I said, interested.

"Well, if I knew what was coming, I could get out of the way of it," he said.

"Simple as that?" I said.

"Simple as that."

Back at Auntie Lizzie's house, I tried to call my mum, but, as usual, she had switched off her phone. So I went to my room, and I took out the sketch of the old man in the bath and the postcard of Kelly the Hen. Time was running out. What was I supposed to do? I needed help, and the only person who could help me — the only person who understood — couldn't even help himself. For Peter, life was just a series of inevitable steps toward death, and there was nothing you could do about it. I wondered what had happened to make him like that. Strange as it sounds, I could feel that he'd been different once. I could sense a warmth and a hope buried in him. I wanted to see it again, though after the fight we'd had, I didn't know if that would ever happen.

Late that night, when everyone else was sleeping, I heard a noise outside the front door. Going down to investigate, I found a package with *Frances* written on the front. I recognized the handwriting from that first postcard I'd delivered. The package was from Peter Kennedy.

TEN

You can understand that I was a bit wary about opening mail from Peter. He had a bad track record for sending post. There was no stamp and no address, so he must have delivered it himself, but when I opened the door, the street was dark and still and empty. No people, no cats. I took the package inside, wondering how he'd found the address of my aunt and uncle. But, of course, he was a messenger. Finding people was what he did.

The package was flat, hard, and wrapped in brown paper. I took it up to my room and opened it. Inside was the painting of the boat at sea. The one I'd seen in his beach hut. Again, I saw how beautiful it was, with the off-center boat and the metal colors of the sky and sea. It reminded me of why I had liked to draw, before the blackouts. At the bottom he'd written, *Just because something is off to the side doesn't mean it's not the point. I'm sorry about this morning, and you're right: I probably am a prick.*

I smiled and suddenly remembered how he had looked on the first night I saw him, stony-faced, with his cigarette and his magnifying glass — his jeweler's loupe — like an eye patch. The long line of him.

There was a letter, too.

Dear Frances,

This is not an excuse. I am a bitter man, and have been for so long that I don't even notice anymore. It has taken you — a very smart girl — to show me what I've become. You said, "Why are you being like this, Peter?" That might have been a rhetorical question, but I thought I might try to answer it, anyway.

When I was eighteen, I met Rowenna Davies, a singer and guitarist in a blues band called the Lifeguards. They played the pubs around Hartsleigh. I'd just moved there. The first time I saw her play, she was magical. She had to flick back her long dark hair to see the guitar. Voice like a glass of cold water on a hot day.

I saw her look at me. I looked better back then. Smarter.

I thought he looked pretty good *now*, in his rugged way.

After the gig, she drank a beer outside. It was summer and warm. I waited until she finished. I felt nervous, because of all the men in her band. But I pulled myself together. "Can I buy you another drink?" I asked.

She looked up with her dark brown eyes and she said,

"Sure. You don't look so bad."

She didn't know how bad I was. How could she?

Of course, I knew the story would not end well.

Being a messenger, I'd come to hate myself, so at first, I couldn't believe Rowenna liked me. Then, a little bit later, I couldn't believe she loved me. But something changed. I changed. Instead of living off my inheritance, I became a plasterer's apprentice. I worked for a man in Helmstown, far enough away that she wouldn't see my curse affecting people she knew in Hartsleigh. I was proud of myself. When I looked in the mirror, or spoke to a customer on the phone, or told her a story or joke, suddenly I could believe that she loved me.

We would play guitar together, long into the night, until the neighbors banged on the wall.

She moved into my flat. I was being reckless and irresponsible, ignoring everything Tabby had taught me. The more I fell in love with Rowenna, the less I was able to leave her, and the more likely I was to paint her. Every day we were together, she was more at risk. If I was painting people I barely even knew, then how long would it be, I wondered, before she turned up in my visions?

For a while, we made it work, but the pressure of being a messenger — and of hiding it — began to get to me. I was moody and nervous. I blacked out at home, and when she asked me what was wrong, I snapped at her.

I had to spend days tracking down recipients, and she became suspicious of my secrecy. She found the names and addresses of strangers — some of them women — in my notebooks. She accused me of having an affair, and when I blacked out, she thought it was because I was drinking. I suppose she just wanted to know what I was hiding, but how could I tell her? How could she believe me? Now we were fighting constantly.

After a while, Rowenna got pregnant. We were so young and I couldn't cope. I imagined how it would be, to black out and wake up with a painting of my own child in my hands. The stakes were too high: I had created a family and — as a messenger — I was sure to destroy it.

One night, Rowenna and I fought, and said things to each other that we shouldn't have. I left. At the time, I thought I was angry with her, but looking back, I knew that I loved her. That was the unbearable thing. I had to ruin it so that I could leave.

I try to be grateful. I had six months of sublime love with Rowenna, and I have a son, even though I don't dare to see him. Every day I try to accept the reality of my situation. Most days I fail. The bitterness seeps in, and I end up behaving like I did when you last came to the beach hut. But the next day, I try again.

All these things are my fault. Your life doesn't have to be as miserable as mine. I didn't listen when Tabby told me to make a life alone. I hoped I would be able to help

you avoid the same mistakes, but I've probably driven
you away as well.

Maybe you're better off without me — most people
are! A messenger's life can be tough, but I wish you well.

Regards,
Peter Kennedy

I lay back on the bed and put the letter over my face.
It smelled of the sea and of the warm wood of the cabin. It
smelled of Peter Kennedy. My breath made the paper damp. I
was sad for him, but I was angry, too. Why did he just accept
things?

The way I felt about Peter was complicated. Half the time
I wanted to kill him, and the other half I wanted to kiss him.
There's only two letters' difference, and I felt like I could go
either way.

On the floor, a dead man stared out at me from my sketch
pad, and I could hear the beginnings of a nasty cough from
Auntie Lizzie's bedroom. The clock was ticking, and I needed
Peter's help. Looking at the letter, I could see that maybe he
needed my help, too.

ELEVEN

I felt pretty wrecked the next day, so I stopped off at the Coffee Shack before going on to Peter's hut. The sketch of the old man was in my bag. The dark-haired guy with the whippet was in front of me in the queue again, and his dog licked my hand. I could feel the nerves coming off the man as he stepped up to order.

"Hello, boy," Helen said, peering over the counter at the dog.

The man stopped himself from answering.

"The usual?"

"Oh. Erm. Yes. Yes, please. Black coffee with —"

"One sugar," said Helen.

I could tell the bloke was flattered that Helen had remembered his order. The whippet tried to put his paws up on the counter. He panted at Helen, who threw him a biscuit, then picked up a foam cup and a black marker.

"What's the name?" she said to the man.

"Hercules," the man said.

"Your name is *Hercules*?" Helen said, frowning.

"No. God, no. I thought you meant the dog. The dog's name is Hercules. My name is Greg."

"Greg, right," Helen said. She wrote on the foam cup with the marker. "It's a new system we're using. It cuts down on confusion at the counter."

"Great," said Greg, scratching his ear. "That's, erm . . . that's great."

Greg wasn't a smooth talker. I noticed that Helen had added *Hercules* under *Greg* on the cup, and drawn a cartoon face of the dog. Greg laughed. "Thank you," he said.

"Bye," said Helen, beaming.

Greg and Hercules went on their way, and I stepped up. "Two teas, please," I said. "My name is Frances."

"What?"

"Frances. So you can write it on the cup?"

"Oh, don't worry about that," Helen said.

I grinned and so did she.

When Peter opened the door, the relief on his face was huge. It made me feel good. He took the teas and my rucksack and offered me his chair. He lit a cigarette.

"You ought to watch that," I said, nodding at the smoke. "It's bad for you."

"Least of my worries."

"No plastering today?" I said.

"Day off. I didn't believe you'd come back after what a terrible waste of space I was yesterday," he said.

74

"Well, I wanted to say thank you for the painting you sent. It's a cracker."

He smiled.

"And I wanted to say thank you for the letter, too."

"I hope it makes me easier to understand."

"Some bits of you," I said. I looked around and noticed that he'd swept the floor and organized his research into piles. He'd shaved, too, and although I liked him with stubble, he seemed rejuvenated.

"You scrub up nice," I said.

"Leave it out," he said, smiling.

"In the spirit of beautifying, I bought you a present from the market." I took the T-shirt out of my rucksack and gave it to him. It was one of those cheap novelty ones. On the front were the words:

WHAT IF THE HOKEY POKEY REALLY IS WHAT IT'S ALL ABOUT?

He held it up and laughed. "I like that. I like that a lot. Thank you."

"I mean, don't get me wrong, the tracksuit top looks great on its own, but it's always nice to have more than one look."

"I get the picture," he said.

He took off his tracksuit top, turning away from me. I watched the muscles in his back as he put on the T-shirt. His forearms were like rope.

"Looks good," I said.

We drank our tea. "You look shattered," he said.

"A lovely thing to say to a girl."

"You know what I mean."

I nodded and took the drawing out of my bag. "Your second present. Not so nice," I said.

He looked at the drawing for a moment and nodded slowly, with sad acceptance. "When did you do it?" he said.

"Day before yesterday. Afternoon."

He looked at his watch. "Why didn't you tell me before?"

"I was too busy calling you a prick," I said.

Peter sighed and studied the page, his face suddenly blank, as if he'd practiced numbing himself to such images — which, I suppose, he had. "Can you remember where you've seen this man?" he said.

"I've never seen him before in my life," I said.

"He lives at Windmill View Retirement Home in Crowdean. His daughter drives him down to the seafront every week. She sits outside the Coffee Shack, and he walks along the path. He likes the sea air."

"You know him?"

"Not really. I see him at Windmill View or when he's walking by. I say *walking* — he has two sticks."

I remembered. I'd nearly knocked him over when I ran away from Peter's hut after that first argument. "How did he get into my head so fast?" I said.

"That's the way it works sometimes," Peter said. "At least we know where he lives."

I looked away, not wanting to think about what was coming. Peter studied the drawing some more. "You're good," he said. "The drawings don't have absolute clarity yet, but that will come. You'll learn to make the images clearer."

"Dead is dead," I said. "What does it matter if the picture looks pretty? Most people only see the shapes anyway."

Peter shrugged. "A sharper image gives you clues as to who the person is. Makes them easier to find. Remember, I tracked Samuel Newman from his number plate."

I thought about that for a while, and then something occurred to me. Something Max had said. *Death is a place. Remove all hazards and obstacles.* I stored that thought for later.

"Shall we go to the retirement home?" Peter said.

"Can't we wait awhile? Why don't we do something else for a bit, to pass the time?"

"Like what?" Peter said.

"Like something that hasn't got to do with anyone dying. You know Helmstown pretty well. What can you do here to relax?"

"You can go mackerel fishing. They take you out into the middle of the sea, and you get to keep what you catch." He sounded excited.

"Peter."

"Yes?"

"That's killing fish."

"Oh. You're right. Well, I know where we can see some living fish."

"Better," I said. "Better."

The Ocean Life Centre was a hundred years old and built under street level. It was like a cave, and they played soft music, which was probably from a CD called *Whale Heaven*, but it got to me. There were eels as long as your arm, with skin like a leopard's. Rocks in the tank suddenly opened their eyes; sea horses fell, seemingly helpless, through the water; and tiny neon fish flashed by like sparks from a bad plug. It was like another world. Just what I needed right then.

Peter had wandered off. I found his silhouette against the bright-green light of a tank. "Look," he said.

There was an ugly brown fish lying flat on a rock, with fins on either side that looked like basic arms. "Oh, yeah," I said. "This is the kind of fish they always show in prehistoric books."

Peter nodded. "The ones that crawl out of the sea and become humans, or whatever. I wonder how long you have to leave them in here before they change."

We laughed.

"The beginnings of life," Peter said.

He disappeared through a curtain and I followed him. It was the jellyfish room. The tanks were glass columns, the darkness broken by a square of light that changed from green to purple to red to blue, making the jellyfish appear to change color, too, as they rose with the slow swish of their skirts. It was magical.

Peter's face went from red to blue, and I admit that I wanted to kiss him. It was as though I could feel the water all around us — in the tanks and in the sea outside — lifting us upward. I closed my eyes and tried to pull myself together, tried to imagine the conversation I might have with Keisha back home:

He's quite soulful, you know. He's had a difficult life, but he's caring underneath it all.

He sounds nice, Fran. How old is he?

He's in his late twenties.

Bit old. What does he do?

Oh, you know. He's a messenger of death.

Ridiculous. I could feel the light changing through my eyelids.

"You OK, Frances?" he asked.

"Yeah, fine," I said, opening my eyes. "Fine. I bet your boy would like this place."

Peter turned away. "I wouldn't know."

"Aren't you curious about him?"

"Of course I am. But it's too dangerous."

"But what if you could — ?"

"I think we've had this conversation."

"Yes, but you had your fingers in your ears," I said.

Peter ignored me, and I decided not to push too hard. We looked at the swaying tentacles of the jellyfish. "They're making me want noodles," I said.

Peter laughed. "Yes, chicken ramen. Let's eat!"

We emerged, squinting, into the sun. We took a shortcut through the museum on our way to the noodle place. There was an exhibition, Cubism to Futurism. That was *all* I needed. But Peter wanted to go in, and I followed him through the door of the cubist room. Straight in front of us was a painting called *Female Nude,* all blocks and shapes.

"So this is the kind of thing that a recipient sees when we show them the message?" I said.

"Apparently. Maybe even more coded and scrambled."

Peter read from the information board on the wall. "'Instead of showing objects from one viewpoint, the cubist artist depicts the subject from many viewpoints to represent it in greater context.'"

"Blah, blah, blah," I said.

The futurism room was scarier, angrier. Crooked cities, melting bodies. There was a sculpture of a man who looked as if he were in the process of exploding.

Again, Peter studied the board. "These futurist guys were mixed up in some nasty stuff," he said. He read aloud: "'The love of danger, violence, patriotism, and war.'"

I spun around, taking in all the distorted shapes and drooping faces. I was becoming dizzy. I kept thinking some violent scene was suddenly going to emerge from the paint. "What's wrong?" Peter said.

"Nothing. Let's go."

As we walked away, I caught sight of a single quote from Pablo Picasso, stenciled onto the wall:

Everything you can imagine is real.

We bought noodles and sat on the bench, watching seagulls peel out of the clouds and perch on the big letters of HELMSTOWN PIER. They looked proud and full of vitality, and they gave me a bit of hope. I looked down at our hands. They had stamped us: OCEAN LIFE. It was an almost perfect afternoon. Or, at least it would have been, had it ended there.

TWELVE

Peter went back to the beach hut and put on a checked shirt. He collected his guitar and an art gallery brochure, and we walked to the bus stop on the grass above the cliffs. He smoked and we talked. I told him about my father and about Johnny being on the run, and he listened. It was the first time I'd really talked to anyone about Johnny's situation.

He told me that when he was nine, his father had gone into hospital for major surgery. There had been complications and a second operation. He'd spent six weeks in intensive care, and it seemed that he wouldn't make it, but somehow he fought back from the brink. The family couldn't believe it — they'd started to accept his death. The doctors had told Peter that his daddy was a miracle man. A week after he came out of hospital, Peter's father slipped and fell down the cellar steps. Peter found the body. He had his first blackout the day after the funeral. "It taught me that there's no meaning in life," he said. "And there is nothing you can do to stop death.

It's inevitable. People think they're in control of their lives, but they're not. Better get used to it."

It occurred to me that we'd both had these God-awful traumatic experiences before our first blackouts — Peter had found his dead father, and I'd watched my brother being beaten to within an inch of his life in front of a crowd of lunatics. I wondered if that was a coincidence.

All I knew was this: the feeling I got, waiting to get on the bus and go to the Windmill View Retirement Home, was not one I planned to get used to. It was sickening.

Peter rolled up the sleeves of his shirt. The bus came and we went up to the top deck. There was nothing but green fields out one window, nothing but blue sea out the other. His leg was next to mine. I could feel the heat of it and wondered if he could feel the heat of mine too. I gripped the seat in front of us.

We got off outside a big old white building that looked like a hospital. "You know where we are?" he said.

I could see the windmill behind the retirement home. "Yes," I said.

"Are you OK?"

I looked at him. "No," I said.

"You will be."

I looked at the windows of the retirement home and saw a shadow pass. "I don't think so," I said. I turned away, but Peter took me by the arm. He was strong. I felt my foot lift off the ground.

"This has to be done. For your sake and for the sake of your family."

"Isn't there some other way?" I said.

"No," Peter said.

"There must be. Don't you understand? This isn't like giving someone a parking ticket. We're talking about death. Doesn't it make you feel . . . desperate?"

Peter sighed. "Yes," he said. He hoisted the strap of his guitar case over his shoulder and carried on walking up the long gravel path.

"They're not going to let us in here anyway," I said. "You have to get permission to visit someone in an old folks' home."

"I can come and go as I please," Peter said.

"How come?"

"I do performances and workshops here in my spare time. I teach painting and sometimes play some songs. It's a good arrangement, because — as you can imagine — I have to come here quite a lot, as a messenger."

I shook my head. "It's sick."

"I've got to deliver the messages. At least this way, I'm giving something back," he said, tapping the guitar case.

"Yeah, you're a real hero. A real guardian of the community. Don't the staff wonder about the fact that every time you turn up, someone dies?"

"It's a nursing home. People die all the time." Peter cleared his throat as we approached the entrance. "Do you have the drawing?" he said.

I shuddered, thinking of the old man lying dead in the bath. "Yes," I said.

Peter rang the doorbell.

"But it's been such a nice day," I said stupidly.

"That's what we do," said Peter. "We ruin people's days."

"You do a lot more than that," I said.

A young woman opened the door. One of the staff. "Peter!" she said. She turned round and shouted back into the next room, where the old folks sat about on brown armchairs. "Everyone, Peter's here!" She said it as if they should be over the moon.

He played a sort of lame country-and-western music, which the oldies loved. They clapped their hands as he sang. I watched him and listened to his fake American accent. The drawing I'd folded into my pocket seemed to be burning a hole through my jeans. I scanned the faces of the old people, and I saw the man from the drawing sitting at the back, grinning with his big white teeth. I thought, strangely, of the windup dentures in Max's room. My stomach did the Big Dipper.

The old folk joined in with the chorus:

"I'm the messenger of love, girl,
And these words I bring to you.
The messenger of love, girl,
But I'm feeling kind of blue.
I'm the messenger of love, girl,
And I need to let you know:
I've searched so hard to find you,
Now I got to let you go."

After the song, the audience broke up. Some of them went to watch TV, while some stayed behind to talk to Peter. The women seemed particularly pleased to see him, especially a woman with big earrings called Jane. I stayed back, not wanting to get involved.

"And who's that with you?" asked Jane, pointing to me.

"That's Frances. She's my apprentice. Soon enough, she'll be visiting care homes on her own."

I nodded and tried to smile, but I was struggling to keep control of my breathing. I tried to think of Maxi's kendo meditation. The man from my drawing was staring out the window.

"Do you do music?" Jane asked me. I shook my head.

"No," said Peter, smiling. "Frances has a talent for drawing. She'll be doing workshops."

Jane laughed and nudged one of her friends. "Ooooh, is it with those nude models?" she said. "What's it called now? Life drawing! Does she do life drawing?"

"The opposite, really," Peter said.

I frowned at him, disgusted.

"What do you mean?" Jane said.

"Landscapes. She does mainly landscapes. Excuse me, ladies," he said, and beckoned me to follow him to where the old man was looking out onto the lawn. I stood shakily and made my way over.

"I'm so sorry, chap, I've forgotten your name," Peter said, sitting down.

"Don't worry, pal," the old man said, winking at me. "Everyone here is forgetful. I wonder what it is about the place. My name's Tom. Tom Kingston."

"You walk down by the seafront sometimes, don't you?"

"I do," said Tom. "Bit of sea air does you good." He leaned forward. "I really only do it so my daughter can get some exercise. Between you and me, she's got a big behind. But she just sits outside that coffee place and eats cake!"

Peter laughed. I fished the drawing from my pocket. I wanted to get it over with. The last thing I needed was get to know the bloke. Peter put his hand on my arm to stop me.

"I hope you don't mind, Tom, but Frances and I brought along this catalog from one of the seafront exhibitions. It's a free gallery, and we thought you might like to visit one day, didn't we, Frances?"

I managed to nod.

Peter passed the catalog to me and kept talking to Tom. I was in a daze and it took me a moment to understand what I was supposed to do. I slipped the folded drawing into the catalog and thrust it toward Tom.

"Here," I said.

"Oh," said Tom. "Right. I don't really need a brochure, to be honest. I can just mosey on down and —"

"Take it," I said, a little abruptly. I softened my voice. "There's some nice pictures in the catalog."

"OK," he said. "Ta."

He flicked through and came to the piece of paper on which I'd drawn his death. "What's this? Oh — you're into that modern art, are you?" he said. He turned the sketch upside down. "It's all just shapes to me. I can't make head nor tail of it. Never have been able to. Now these sea views, that's more my style. . . ." He slipped the piece of paper back into the catalog and continued reading. "I'll take this upstairs, if I may," he said. "Now, if you'll excuse me, I must do my ablutions before the ladies use up all the hot water."

Peter helped him stand and get his canes, and then Tom Kingston crept down the corridor with his four-step rhythm, the brochure clasped between his elbow and his body. I felt Peter's hand cover mine, and I had to hold back the tears.

One of the old ladies, seeing how distressed I looked, got me a cup of tea, and they crowded around me, asking what was wrong, but I couldn't speak.

"She's all right," Peter said. "She's had a tough day, that's all."

Part of me wanted to punch him, but the other part—the bigger part—wanted to lean against his strong shoulder. So I did.

"This is how I was in the beginning," he whispered.

After a while, a noise like a dinosaur came from the ceiling, a screeching and rumbling that made the walls quake. "What's that?" Peter said.

"It's the old Victorian water pipes," Jane said.

Tom Kingston was running his final bath.

THIRTEEN

We left before they found him.

On the bus home, I didn't really want to talk about what had happened at the care home, but I knew that when I got back to Auntie Lizzie's, I wouldn't be able to.

"He was a nice man," I said. "Why did he have to be such a nice man?"

"They're the easiest. The toughest ones are the bad people," Peter said.

"What?" I said. "How can you possibly say that?"

"It's worse, believe me. When they're bad, there's a part of you that wants to do it, and that's hard to live with. Eventually, you'll stop feeling anything and things will get better."

"Why do you think it's better not to feel?" I said. "Feeling stuff is important. It makes you want to change the situation. I don't want to be someone with no emotions."

I was trying to provoke him, but he just shrugged and looked out to sea. I thought about the future. If I was only going to draw people I had seen, then maybe I should hang around in prisons, with the pedos and murderers. But then I thought of Johnny. He could be in prison soon. I'd neglected Johnny recently. All the stuff with Peter had taken over my life.

From the bus window, I looked back at the windmill. I thought of the little plastic beach windmills I'd seen on the pier.

We passed a road sign. HARTSLEIGH 15 MILES.

"If you could control your gift, would you see your son?" I said.

"I don't believe it can be controlled. Tabby knew so much about the folklore and history of the messengers. She didn't think there was any way round it. She told me it was probably dangerous to even try," Peter said.

"And you just believed her?" I said.

"She was like a parent to me."

"And you never questioned your parents?"

"Look, it's too risky. I believe that death is bigger than us. It's a force we can't underst—"

"Oh, whatever," I said. "I'm sick of this moping, mystic rubbish."

I was fed up. I hate it when people won't try to help themselves. But when I looked at Peter again, he was almost crying. I realized he'd been trying to tell me about his mentor—about his feelings for her—but I hadn't really been listening.

"How did Tabby die?" I said.

"I killed her," he said instantly. He regained his composure. His face became unreadable again. He'd learned to bury his emotions. He'd had to.

"You painted her?"

"Yes."

"And you *delivered* the message? I thought you said she was everything to you."

"She was. I didn't deliver the message."

"So how come she died?"

He closed his eyes. "Tabby called it the *double bind*. She'd told me about it, you see. I think she knew it was coming. Sometimes you draw a person you love. If you deliver the message, they die. If you don't, they die anyway, because you didn't deliver the message. That's the double bind."

"Jesus," I said.

"She told me about it, but I didn't believe her. When I painted her, I burned the message. But it still came to pass. *That's* why I feel like I don't have much choice about the way things turn out."

We didn't speak for the rest of the journey.

His gift to me, when I left the bus, was a stack of blank postcards. "For your next messages. Makes things simpler," he said. When I took them, I was accepting what I had become: a messenger.

Back at the house, I survived Uncle Robert's cheerful questions about my day, and I survived Auntie Lizzie's kindness and concern. They'd saved some food, which I ate in the kitchen, but my mind kept drifting to Tom Kingston with his sticks, walking down the hallway at Windmill View.

I went to my room as soon as I could. I knew Johnny would have helped. I'd have been able to tell him about being a messenger, and he'd have taken it seriously. I pulled back the curtains and whispered out onto the dusty blue streets: *"Where are you?"*

I hoped he wasn't living rough. God, I wanted him back, even if it meant he might end up in jail. I knew that was selfish, though. Maybe he'd be better off running away completely, taking a plane to South America or someplace. Sometimes, when I closed my eyes, I saw the policeman in intensive care. Other times, the face behind the breathing equipment was Johnny's.

There was no point sitting there wallowing. I remembered a girl I knew at school, from my art class, whose dad was a lawyer. I took out my mobile and called. She answered, sounding the same as always, half-really-interested but half-doing-something-else. *"Frances?* Oh, hey! Not seen you for a while."

"I've been away for the summer. Listen, I've got this . . . this legal question. You probably know about my brother. . . ."

"Your brother?" she said, and I waited for the penny to drop. It did. "Oh, yeah, right. Your brother."

"I just wondered if I might be able to ask your dad a quick question about his case."

She was quiet for a moment and then told me to hang on. She covered the phone with her hand, though I could still hear her whispering. *"Yeah, the one who punched the policeman. . . . No, not really. She's in my art class. . . . OK."*

"Hi, Frances?" she said.

"Yeah."

"He's not in."

We exchanged quick good-byes and then I hung up. You can be the most determined person in the world. You can be a doer and a go-getter who powers through the obstacles of life and goes on about being in control of her own destiny. But sometimes you can look at your own family and think, *This is a mess and I just don't know how to clean it up.*

Later that night, my mind was still crackling, so I decided to give Maxi's meditation another go. I sat on the end of the bed and closed my eyes, tensed each muscle and then released. I felt the warm tingle. A few minutes later, I heard a noise. It was the sound of the sea. That was impossible. Even if Uncle Robert hadn't bought the best double-glazing in the world, I still shouldn't have been able to hear the sea. It was miles away. But there it was, crashing and fizzing in my head.

The waves started to wash all the other thoughts away: Tom Kingston, Pete and Rowenna playing guitar together, Johnny pounding the streets . . . All those images disappeared under the hissing of the water. The noise was like a silence.

I don't know how long I sat there, but when I came round, I knew what I had to do. I was a messenger, but that didn't mean I had to accept everything Peter said about it. You must deliver the message or your loved ones will suffer, he had said. But he hadn't mentioned anything about what I could or couldn't do *after* the message had been delivered.

I thought back to the cubist paintings and what Peter had read from the information board. *The cubist artist depicts the subject from many viewpoints to represent it in greater context.* That's what a death was: it was a context with many viewpoints. It was a coming together of lots of different elements. But what if I could change one of those elements? What if I could mess around with the context? *"Remove anything hazardous,"* Maxi had said.

I took the postcard of Kelly the Hen out of my rucksack and went to Uncle Robert's study. Everyone had gone to bed; the house was quiet. I fired up the computer, plugged in the scanner, and scanned the postcard. The program told me the image wasn't recognized, but it came up fine on the monitor. The screen was a twenty-four-incher, so I had a good view of Peter's painting. The detail was incredible, especially considering that the postcard was so small.

I zoomed in on the stretcher by the ambulance. I could see Kelly's nose, some blood around it, and a fluorescent green liquid staining her cheek. I could see the veins in her arm. I zoomed in on the faces of the people surrounding the ambulance. Everyone was in fancy dress. There were a few of Kelly's cowgirl friends and a big hefty bloke dressed as a schoolgirl, who looked very worried. The detail of the painting was so sharp, I could see the clumps of his mascara.

The cause of Kelly's death was unclear. Had she fallen? Was it drink or drugs? Maybe she just had a heart attack, and what was I supposed to do about that? Well, I couldn't do anything until I'd figured out where she was. I scrolled around the painting, looking for clues. The ambulance was parked outside a bar called the Pink Barracuda. I scribbled the name onto a Post-it. At the top of the road, in the background, was a clock tower. Surely, I thought, there was no way he could get that sort of detail. But then I remembered the loupe he wore over his eye when he was checking the postcards for clues. I zoomed in. Amazing. I could see both clock hands with perfect clarity. A quarter to three. I looked at the clock in the corner of the computer screen. It was 1:34. No time to hang around. I got out my kit bag and took some of the cash that Mum had given me.

I stopped when I got to Max's room. I always gave the impression I was a tough girl, but for this mission I wanted company.

His hand rose to his face when I hit the light switch, but somehow he kept on sleeping. His toe was sticking out of the covers, so I pinched it. "What the bloody hell—?" he said. He reached out for his glasses and put them on. "You again. Cousin, this is a bad habit, you waking me up. It's not going to deepen our friendship."

"Fancy a beer?" I said.

"Are you crazy? No. I'm in training. What I eat and drink is training. When I sleep, it's training."

"How about some drugs?" I said.

"Go to bed," he said.

"I need to go into town. It's really important."

"How important?"

I realized what he was after. Money for his kendo kit. "It's probably worth a face mask," I said.

"They're three hundred pounds," he said.

"It's worth ten percent of a face mask."

"Fifteen percent."

"Done," I said, taking out my fold of notes and peeling a few off. Maxi slapped his forehead when he saw how much cash I had.

"You should have asked for twenty-five percent," I said.

"We'll have to be quiet," Maxi said, climbing out of his bed. He had a bit of a tent in his shorts, and he didn't quite turn away in time.

"Lordy, Max! You'll make me blush!" I said.

I won't repeat what he said in reply, but it wasn't up to his usual standard of good manners.

Helmstown was a big, beautiful mess. A blur of bright lights and bright clothes and bare flesh. There was some sort of football tournament that summer, and people had been drinking all day. Everything was red and white and flashing—even the people. "Where's the clock tower?" I said.

Maxi, who was used to hanging around in dark bedrooms and on dark seafronts, turned his nose up. "You don't want to go there."

"I have to," I said.

"It's like the end of the world."

"I don't care."

He shook his head and pointed the way. "What's this all about, anyway?" he said.

"Nothing. It's no big deal. I met this woman today. We got

on well, and she invited me out with her friends."

"No big deal," Maxi said. "You dragged me out of bed and it's *no big deal.*"

"Look. There'll be at least ten women there, and they will all be up for it. Honestly, you should be grateful."

Great Western Street ran from the clock tower down to the seafront, and it was stag and hen night central. *"The end of the world,"* Maxi had said.

"They're just having . . . fun," I said, watching a man dressed as Fred Flintstone puke into a drain.

We marched down to the Pink Barracuda. The doorman eyed us suspiciously. Maybe because we were underage or maybe because we weren't dressed like we'd covered ourselves in wallpaper paste and run through the thrift store. But he let us in.

The bar was rammed, and I struggled through the crowds to where Kelly and her gang were drinking tequila shots, still wearing their cowboy hats. Kelly had three shots in front of her.

"There they are!" I shouted in Maxi's ear.

"Those women? And you thought *my* friends were bad."

"Your friends don't wear enough cowboy gear."

"This place is revolting," he said.

"Don't be such a mard-arse," I said.

I intentionally bumped into Kelly from behind and then apologized. "'S OK," she said. I stared into her eyes. She was already very drunk. I didn't know exactly how she was going to die, but I was beginning to lean toward alcohol as a cause. I remembered the green liquid on her face in the message. She frowned at me.

"Hello," I said.

"Haven't I seen you before?" she said.

"Don't think so," I said, hoping she wouldn't remember me slapping the postcards out of her hand. "Is it your hen night?"

"Yup," she said, swaying slightly. "I'm getting married next week."

"How romantic," I said. "What's his name?"

"Steve," she said, slurring the word slightly so it sounded like *sleeve.* "We were destined to be together."

"How did he propose?"

"On the London Eye. Thirty-first of December."

"New Year's Steve!" I said.

She screamed with laughter. "You're funny, you are," she said. "Here, have a shot. I don't think I can manage all three."

"Thanks," I said. I picked one of the tequilas up and knocked the other two over with my elbow.

"Oh, sorry," I said.

While she was staring at the mess, I tipped the third one on the floor. I needed to be sober. A couple of the other women looked daggers at me.

"Sorry," I said again. "Kelly, let me get you another drink. Come with me to the bar."

"Erm, who are you again?" she said.

"Frances!" I said, as if I was really offended that she'd forgotten.

"And you're going to buy me a drink?"

"Of course."

She looked confused for a moment, but then she shrugged. "OK," she said.

I turned around to introduce her to Max, but he was doing the lasso dance with one of the other cowgirls. She was a bit younger and prettier than the others, and she looked like a pixie. I laughed and Kelly laughed too. I looked at my watch. It was 2:15 a.m. Unless I could do something about it, Kelly had thirty minutes to live.

At the bar, I tried to let as many people go before me as I could, to give Kelly time to sober up. She was rocking on her feet and kept bumping into me. She wasn't a small woman, and I wondered if I'd be able to carry her out if it came to that. She kept looking back at the other girls, who had started to mingle with a group of rugby lads in drag. I recognized the one dressed as a schoolgirl from the painting. My heart jumped. "What do you want to drink, Kelly?" I said. "How about a water? It's good to hydrate your skin before the wedding."

"Water? No, thanks. I . . . I . . . I'm here to . . . enjoy meself. I'll have a woman pope . . . I mean . . . a rum and Coke."

It could have been worse—the bar had an offer on absinthe. I bought a couple of Cokes without rum. She took a big gulp but didn't notice the lack of alcohol. I started asking her questions about the wedding dress and her family and the bridesmaids. It seemed to help her concentrate. The problem was, as she sobered up, she started to wonder why she was talking to a girl she didn't know. She began to look around, frowning.

Then, before I knew what was happening, we were surrounded by cowgirls and rugby players. "Kel, Kel, Kel!" one of the older women said. "We've got another *dare* for you." The other girls whooped. "You've got to get your boobs out for one of these men!"

The big guy from the painting was laughing, his pigtails flung back. "Yeah," he said. "Come on."

She won't do it, I thought. But she did. It was only for a second, but cheers and screams went up. *Poor old Steve,* I thought. Getting your boobs out was obviously a decent way to meet men, because pretty soon Mr. Schoolgirl was whispering in her ear. I tried to go over and speak to her, but the other girls blocked me off. "Let her have a bit of fun," one of them said.

"Yeah," said another one. "What's it got to do with you? Who *are* you, anyway?"

One of the rugby lads put his thick sweaty hand on my waist. "Where are *your* cowboy boots, darling?" he said.

"I'm wearing trainers, and you'll have one of them embedded in your shinbone if you don't get your hands off me," I said.

"Oh, come on," he said.

I sidestepped him, but I couldn't see Kelly anymore, and we were running out of time. I spun round, looking for a cowboy hat, but there were too many of them. I started to panic. A word came into my head, spoken in Peter's voice. That word was *inevitable.*

Eventually I spied Kelly at the edge of the dance floor, near Max and the pixie girl. Mr. Schoolgirl was standing next to her, holding two plastic test tubes of liquid. It was absinthe. And it was green. I knew that the absinthe would tip her over the edge. Kelly was shaking her head, saying no, but Mr. Schoolgirl was reasoning with her. She leaned against him, hardly able to stand up by herself. I tried to push toward them, but the place was too crowded. It felt like there were hands all over me. Kelly took the test tube, and I flashed back to the painting. The green stains on her face. "Kelly!" I shouted, but the music was so loud I could barely hear my own voice.

And then this happened: Mr. Schoolgirl shouted something to the pixie girl. She smiled. Max was smiling, too, and then, all of a sudden, he wasn't. Mr. Schoolgirl had grabbed the pixie's behind. I hardly saw what Maxi did, he was so fast. But suddenly, Mr. Schoolgirl was on the floor, and there was green drink everywhere.

A few screams rang out over the music, and the crowd moved away from the center of the scene. I struggled over. Max had his knee in the big guy's back and his pigtails in his hand. The wig came off and the big bloke's head smacked the floor.

"Max!" I shouted. "You OK?"

He looked up at me, almost surprised by what had happened, as if he'd done it without thinking. "Yeah. A damn sight better than this guy, anyway."

"Ow, get off!" the big bloke screamed, and I told him to shut it. Words were had, and a few seconds later, two bouncers were dragging everyone outside.

The sea air was very welcome. One of the bouncers started pushing Maxi around, and I went over. "Look at the size of him compared to you," I said. "You should be ashamed of yourself."

The bouncer left Maxi and moved on to help his colleague, who was roughing up Mr. Schoolgirl. Maxi smiled at me.

"Having a good night?" I said.

"Not too bad," Max said. "It's like training. Sort of."

He spotted the pixie girl, and they started talking again, away from the crowd.

Kelly was confused. She looked down at her white shirt, which now had a green bib of absinthe. It looked like none of the liquid had made its way into her mouth. In the quiet of the street, I could hear the world again. Little beeps went off, a few seconds apart. Hour alarms. I looked at my watch, and then up at the clock tower at the top of the road.

Three a.m.

"Yes!" I shouted. "I did it! We did it!"

I grabbed Kelly and hugged her tight. "You're OK, Kelly! You're going to make it."

Kelly was weeping. Drunk. The drunk weeping phase. "Me blouse," she said. "It's bloody ruined."

I stroked her arm, felt her living flesh against my fingers. "Cheer up, Kelly," I said. "Could have been worse."

FOURTEEN

Max and me crashed in the living room that night, each on our own massive sofa. Cheese and piccalilli sandwiches, cups of tea. "I can see the future, Maxi," I said.

"So can I. You're going to spill your tea. And then we're going to get a roasting from Mum."

"No, I'm serious. I can actually see the future. And I can change it."

He asked what I had asked. What anyone would ask. "What's going to happen to me, then?"

"I don't ever want to see *your* future, Maximum," I said.

But now it didn't matter if I did. I thought I'd worked it all out. I could still deliver the message, so my family would be safe, but I had found a way to cheat death. Peter had almost convinced me that the death of a recipient was inevitable, but I had fought against the way he accepted things. I was just angry that I hadn't thought of it before I let Tom Kingston go for his bath.

I lay back into the soft cushions and pondered what all of this could mean for me, and for Peter and his son. I thought of

Peter's face, red and then blue in the jellyfish room. I thought about his big arm around my waist in the retirement home, the way it made my heart beat faster to be pulled toward him.

That night I dreamed of Nana's house in Whiteslade, where I'd woken from my first blackout. I still didn't know why that night kept sneaking into my mind. I dreamed that I was running away from Johnny, his face swollen and shiny after the fight. I ran through Nana's living room, through the kitchen with its lino that stuck to my feet, out into the garden, over the stone wall, and toward the shed, with a blank sheet of paper flapping in my hand. Mum was shouting to me, and Johnny was too. "I'm OK," he was saying. "Look. It's only a few scratches. I'm going to be OK."

It wasn't the worst nightmare I'd ever had. You might even say it was reassuring, what with Johnny telling me he would be fine. But Johnny had always lied to make people feel better. And there was this feeling in the dream, something at the edges of my mind. A feeling of something horrible coming.

When I woke up, I remembered a conversation Johnny had had with one of them God squad people who knock on your door.

The woman asked Johnny what he did for a living, and when he answered, she told him that boxing was a sin.

"Oh, aye?" he'd said. "How come?"

"The Bible says, 'Do unto others as you would have them do unto you.'"

"What if you wake up one morning and all you want them to do is give you a beating?"

The woman hadn't known what to say, and Johnny had slowly closed the door, smiling.

I'd been hiding round the corner, and it was a big moment for me. For all those years of boxing, I'd never thought that he'd actually *wanted* to be hit.

I thought about it now, and I was scared for him.

Me running away from Johnny. Johnny running away from everyone. I hoped it wouldn't be like this forever.

Until I saved Kelly the Hen, I hadn't realized how much becoming a messenger had changed me. So much of my life before had been about *looking* at things. I loved to sketch, to watch movies, to watch people. I always won staring contests. But now I avoided eye contact because I was afraid people might seep into my messages. I'd started to look at the ground, like a geisha. When you're a messenger, looks can kill.

But now that I'd saved Kelly, a fragile bit of hope came back to me. On my way to Peter's hut the next morning, I was able — tentatively — to hold my head up again.

He was waiting with tea from the Coffee Shack. "The new Peter Kennedy," I said, sitting down. "His chest is covered, and there's no plaster on his jeans."

"Frances! Always a pleasure. And that was almost a compliment. You seem to be feeling better than when we left Windmill View," he said.

My head dropped. I wasn't ready for the reminder.

"I'm sorry," he said. "That was insensitive. I forget, sometimes, what it's like at the beginning. Things'll get easier."

"I know," I said, and he seemed puzzled by my sudden brightness. I wanted to keep my secret for a little bit longer, so I changed the subject. "Hey, where do you live when you're not at the beach hut?"

"Little flat in town."

"What happened to the place you lived in with Rowenna?"

He sighed. "I gave it to her. I made sure the paperwork was in order. I didn't want them to be homeless. I send child support money. I just don't give a return address. . . ." He trailed off.

"So you moved out and got a new place."

"It was a while before I bought the flat."

"What happened after you moved out?"

"What's this—twenty questions?" he snapped. But then he sighed and sat down on his chair. "I lost my mind a bit," he said.

"What do you mean?"

"I couldn't take it. The situation. Being a messenger had ruined my chance of happiness with Ro. It had ruined my life. I was frightened that if I could remember Rowenna's face, it might end up in one of my paintings. I'd already killed Tabby, and I couldn't risk it happening again. I tried to wipe Rowenna out of my memory."

"What did you do?"

"I drank. I stayed in a bed-and-breakfast for a while, but they soon kicked me out. Half of the time I was drunk; the other half I was trying to track people down and deliver the messages so that Rowenna and my son would be safe."

"Sounds dark," I said.

"To say the least. So, it was obvious what would happen."

"What?"

"I ended up in an institution."

"You went insane?" I said.

"That's not a word I like. I was sick — that's all. Really sick. Of course, nobody there was bothered that I was banging on about how I was a messenger and I could paint death. Everyone was saying something like that, in there. They just gave me more pills."

"How did you get better?"

"The medicine numbed my feelings and made me forget. Eventually Rowenna's face faded from my memory."

He stopped for a moment and took a long breath before continuing. "And so she was safe," he said, and smiled. "Which was good."

"I suppose. Not exactly ideal, though, is it?"

"Nothing about being a messenger is ideal, Frances. It changes you. There is death everywhere. And it can be painful. If you get too close to people, you can destroy them, and yourself."

I looked over his desk: the phone books and the jeweler's loupe glinting in the sun coming through the crack in the door. "I think I might have found a way to change all that," I said.

And I told him the story of how I'd saved Kelly the Hen.

FIFTEEN

"You did *what*?" he said.

"I stopped it from happening. Well, Max stopped it, really, but—"

Peter smashed his fist into the desk, and I jumped.

"What's wrong with you?" I said.

"Don't you see what you've done? This could be a disaster. You don't know what you're dealing with. This is unknown territory! Every piece of knowledge that has been passed down points to the fact that death has an order."

"Oh, garbage," I said.

"It's a stupid risk. We have to stick to what little we know. We have to play it safe. If Tabby taught me one thing, it's that you can mess with life all you want, but you *cannot* mess with death."

"Doctors do it all the time," I said.

"No! You don't know that." He was on his feet now. "What if, when a doctor *supposedly* saves someone, it's because that person wasn't ready to die? That's what *I* believe. That's what I've learned from being a messenger: death is mapped out. You can't reason with it, and you can't stop it. It's a force of nature, and it takes whatever is in its way."

"That's a cop-out, Peter. That's just an excuse to sit back and do nothing. People can make a difference in the world. People can change things. We have a choice."

"Who the hell are you to imagine that you have any control over life and death?" Peter said.

"Well, I obviously do, because I saved Kelly."

"And at what price? At what price? Eh?" He crouched down to me, shouting in my face, and I wondered if he was losing it. After all, he just told me he'd spent time in an institution. "Do you have any idea about the consequences of what you've done?" he said.

"No. Do you?" I said.

"That's . . . I . . ."

"You don't, do you?"

"I . . . Tabby warned me about this. She said it was the unbreakable rule."

"And you're saying you never tried it? Not once?"

"Of course I didn't! Tabby made it perfectly clear that—"

"Who was Tabby, anyway? What made her such an authority on everything?"

"Don't you dare doubt her! Besides, the stakes are too high to mess about. You can't just *try things*. My family—"

"But *you* showed Kelly the postcard," I said. "*You* delivered the message. By your logic, nothing will happen to your family."

"What about *yours*?" he said. "You have put the people you love in terrible jeopardy."

For some reason, that made me snap. "The people I love are already in jeopardy! I've got a nervous wreck of a mum who won't even talk to me. The bloody police are hunting down my brother like an animal. And God only knows where my dad is. As for me, if I have to spend the rest of my life as a murderer, then I'd rather be dead."

Peter looked shocked. *Good*, I thought. I marched out of his hut and slammed the door.

That night, I sat with Auntie Lizzie in the living room. On the TV, detectives were gathered at crime scenes where the murders had already happened. Maybe, I thought, I didn't need Peter. What good had he done me so far? I tried to convince myself I could get through it all on my own.

At about nine p.m., I started to feel tired. It seemed like the furniture was suddenly too big, as if the sofa might swallow me up. So I said good night to Auntie Lizzie and went upstairs. I began to feel woozy before I got to the top, and I blacked out on the landing. The next few minutes were oblivion, and when I woke up in the trancelike state, I pulled a postcard and a pencil from my rucksack, and I drew the message there and then.

I must have fallen asleep on the landing, because Uncle Robert found me at around eleven p.m., huddled over the postcard.

"Frances?" he whispered. "Are you OK?"

"Fine," I said. "I'm fine."

"What are you doing?"

"Nothing," I said.

I covered the postcard, although he'd only have seen a jumble of shapes anyway. Still, he looked at me suspiciously. In fact, he almost looked afraid. I wondered about what I was becoming.

"Right. OK, then," he said, walking off to the bathroom.

In my bedroom, I looked at what I'd drawn.

A streetlight in an alleyway.

A woman lying on the ground, blood across her face.

There was a rolled-up bundle by her legs and the contents of a Sainsbury's shopping bag scattered around her body.

Four youths were leaving the scene.

I needed Peter. I had no idea how to read the message, no idea where the death would take place, and no idea how to stop it from happening. I needed him because—although I never would have admitted it—I was frightened. And I needed him because he quickened my pulse and made me feel alive.

Then I looked closer at the woman in the picture. Beneath the wounds, I recognized her and my heart jumped.

It was Helen from the Coffee Shack.

I had my pride. So it wasn't like I went banging on his door.

But I spent most of the next morning sitting on one of the metal chairs outside the Coffee Shack, watching Helen serve the customers, and storm clouds rolling in over the sea.

Peter came and found me. He stood at my table. "Can I sit down?"

"Not if you're going to bang on about how irresponsible I am."

"I won't. But I do need to say something. You shouldn't have said you'd rather be dead. You're a good person, and you've got a lot to live for."

"Well," I said. "I suppose you can sit down, then."

He did. "I'm sorry about how I reacted," he said.

"It's OK. But don't you see what it could mean, if we can save people? For you? For both of us?"

I knew he was thinking of his son. I could see that it caused him pain. He shook his head and lit a cigarette. "I suppose I've accepted the situation for so long that it seemed easier to go on accepting it. There's nothing more painful than . . ."

"Hope?" I said.

"Yes," he said.

I put my hand on his arm.

"How did you find the clues, again?" he said.

"I scanned the painting onto a computer and enlarged it. The image is so small, but I could zoom in and move around, looking for what might have happened. Your paintings have such detail, so that helped."

"I've been doing it for a long time."

"Pete, this could set you free from all the pain you have to witness. And it could mean you're able to see your family again. You could meet your boy. Even if you paint him, God forbid, you'll be able to work out how to stop it from happening."

"That's a huge risk," he said.

He was imagining it — imagining himself painting the death of his son, the horror of waking up to it. He was imagining himself showing the painting to the boy, and the panic of trying to work out what was going to happen.

"It would be worth it though, wouldn't it?" I said.

"For me perhaps."

"For the bloody recipients!" I said.

"Well, yes," he said. "They obviously stand to benefit."

"And for your boy, too. He'd have a dad. Better than that," I said. "He'd have you."

"Maybe I could just see him a couple of times," Peter said. "Just to meet him."

"Yes! See how it goes."

He took a deep breath. "I think the computer zoom might be better than my loupe," he said. "Will you show me how to scan the pictures and search them?"

"Of course. Don't you have a scanner?" I said.

"No."

"We can go to the library."

He stood up.

"Peter," I said, taking the postcard of Helen from my rucksack. "We can start with this."

He turned his head and squinted at the pencil sketch. "Hey, isn't that . . . ?" He turned to look at the serving counter of the Coffee Shack.

"Yes," I said.

"When did you draw it?"

"Last night."

"Jesus," he said. "Let's get going."

We rushed off to the library. A car slowed down on the main road, and I immediately winced, as if an accident would follow.

The messenger instinct. But nobody died this time, and the man in the car was Uncle Robert. I made eye contact briefly, but Robert was more concerned with the tall man at my side.

"We'll have to get one of those computers in the corner of the room," I said. Of course, being the area of a public library used mainly by people who didn't have home Internet access, it was full of folk who looked weirder than us, doing things that were only slightly less dodgy.

We waited for a bloke with half a skinhead to stop scanning the palms of his hands, and then we moved in and got to work. I showed Peter how to upload the image of the postcard, and we waited some more. I flinched when it opened. I didn't know Helen beyond buying a cup of tea from her, but it was still hard to see her like that, her face bloodied.

Peter was calm. He'd seen this sort of thing so many times before. "Our job is to work out her final movements," he said. "How do I zoom in?"

I showed him.

He swept across the picture, zeroing in on certain details: the streetlight, the trainers of one of the youths leaving the scene, Helen's face, the Sainsbury's carrier bags. He muttered to himself. Eventually, he focused on the rolled-up bundle by her knee.

"What's that?" I said.

"Looks like a yoga mat," said Peter.

"So, that's a clue! She goes to yoga."

"This is Helmstown," Peter said. "There are approximately ten million yoga classes."

"So how do we find out which one she goes to?" I said.

"We use an old-fashioned research method," Peter said.

"What's that?"

"We talk to her. You're going to ask her where she does her class."

"Why me?"

"You have a rapport with her," Peter said. It was true. And it was what made this message so scary.

We stared at the screen a little longer. "You need to speak to her as soon as possible and get as much information as you can. A street name at least," he said.

I felt suddenly nervous about the prospect of speaking to Helen.

"Could we not just tell her what's going to happen?" I said.

"What, you mean go up to her and say, 'Excuse me, I wouldn't go to yoga tomorrow night, because you're going to die on the way back'?"

"She wouldn't believe us," I said.

"She'd have us locked up," Peter said. "I should know. If we're going to do this sort of thing, we need to stay under the radar."

I nodded. "OK. I'll speak to her. I'll do it when I deliver the message."

"Today," he said.

"She'll have finished her shift. I'll do it tomorrow." I paused. "Peter."

"Yes."

"I can't look at this anymore. I feel sick," I said.

"OK," he said, taking the postcard out of the scanner and clicking the *X* to close the window. "Let's call it a day. I'll go back to the Coffee Shack and see what I can find out about her from the other staff. You need some rest."

We left the library and emerged into a gray, humid headache of an afternoon. "I have to go back to my auntie's," I said.

"Yes," Peter said. He looked at me.

"Y'all right, mate?" I said.

He put his arms around me, and I let myself enjoy the nearness of him. I put my hand on his chest, and he didn't move it away. I felt this weight, this urge, pulling me toward him. I couldn't get near enough. "Thank you, Frances," he said. "I'm not sure I'm comfortable about messing with fate yet. We'll have to keep an eye on the consequences. . . ."

I sighed.

"But thank you for trying," Peter said.

"That's OK," I said. "You owe me, though."

He said something else as he turned to go. It sounded like "You're amazing," but I couldn't be sure. Since Johnny had gone, I hadn't heard those sort of words much.

I walked around the block a couple of times. I called Mum, I called Johnny, but I couldn't get an answer. I felt like I had a lot of energy, a lot of power, and it had to go somewhere. So I made sure Peter had left the area, and then I went back into the library, to the local studies section. I took a piece of scrap paper, sat down at a computer with a couple of telephone directories, and began to search for Peter's son.

SIXTEEN

The next day, I went to the beach as early as I could. The life of Helen, a coffee waitress in her twenties, was in our hands. We had until about 9:15 p.m. that night to save her. I walked toward the Coffee Shack and stood back for a moment. They had a Saint George flag on the shack, because of the football tournament, but without much wind, the cross on the flag had drooped and looked more like an *X*. Helen's red hair was tied back, and steam from the kettle rose around her face. I got in line. Greg, the man with the whippet, was there again. The guy drank so much coffee, it was a wonder his brain didn't explode.

"You know, *I* have a dog," Helen said as she got his drink.

"Do you? Great! I mean, what kind?"

"A Weimaraner."

"Oh, they're nice."

"Same color as Hercules, just about."

"Yes?"

"Sort of milky coffee."

"No. Black, please. One sugar."

Helen laughed. I could see that Greg was working hard to build up some courage. "Actually," he said, "Hercules and I often walk the route beneath the cliffs. It's really beautiful, and he loves it. There's a nice café at the end. . . ."

"Really?" said Helen, looking hopeful as she handed him his cup.

"Yes," he said. He paused and seemed to lose his confidence. "Anyway, thanks for the coffee. Bye."

He turned and walked away, his eyes shut tight and a grimace on his face. Even Hercules looked forlorn.

Helen was clearly disappointed. But she didn't know what was coming next, did she? I felt sick, but I tried not to show it. "Hello. Two teas, please," I said.

"That's two pounds twenty," she said.

I put the postcard in front of her on the counter and watched her eyes flicker over it. "That's nice. Is it Picasso?"

"Oh, sorry," I said. I replaced the postcard with a five-pound note.

"Thank you," she said.

"Hey, do you do yoga?" I said.

"Yes, how did you know? Is it because I'm so flexible and relaxed?" she said, laughing.

"I saw you with your mat the other day," I said. "Anyway, I've been thinking of going to classes."

"Really? Well, I go to the Ashtanga place on Ferris Avenue. The teacher is really good, and she doesn't make you do too much of the embarrassing chanting."

"What time do you go?"

"I do the eight-till-nine-o'clock class. I'm going tonight actually."

"Great," I said. "I might see you there."

I took the drinks and a long look at Helen, then made my way back to the beach hut.

Peter was ready with a map of Helmstown, his laptop, and a pile of notes. I saw that he'd bought a scanner, too.

"OK. So, tonight she goes to yoga. Then she shops at Sainsbury's, and then she goes home to Butler Street," Peter said.

The previous day, Peter had struck up a conversation with the manager of the Coffee Shack. He'd pretended to know Helen and found out her surname, which was Rossdale. From that information, he'd found out where she lived.

We looked at the map, trying to figure out which alley I had drawn in the message.

"There's a Sainsbury's near her house," I said, pointing to the map.

"Yes, but if she goes to yoga *here*, on Ferris Avenue, then she'd go to the Sainsbury's *here*, because it's right next door."

I followed her probable route home with my finger and found a thin street. "Vine Alley," I said. "She'd go down Vine Alley."

"I know where that is," he said.

"But it's safer to stall her outside the yoga class, isn't it?" I said.

"Not necessarily. We don't know how long those kids

will hang around. Let's meet here, and then walk to the alley together. Her class finishes at nine, so let's meet at eight thirty, just to be safe."

The determined expression he'd had for the last half hour suddenly slipped into one of doubt as he looked at the screen.

"What's wrong?" I said.

"They'll probably just beat up someone else," Peter said.

"We can only do what we can," I said. "We've got the opportunity to save someone, and we've got to take it."

"We don't really know anything about this woman," Peter said. "Who's to say she's a good person? She could be a mass murderer, for all we know."

"I doubt many mass murderers do yoga," I said.

"I'm just saying. There are always consequences."

"I know that. The difference between you and me is that you always think the consequences are going to be terrible."

"So would you if you'd been a messenger for as long as I have. It's a result of personal experience."

"Well, let's start making some good experiences, shall we?"

He stared at the wall of his hut, mulling it all over. "OK," he said eventually. "I'll see you tonight."

Auntie Lizzie tried to smile when I got home, but I could tell something was on her mind. She was tense. Decent people like her are rubbish at hiding how they feel. "Oh, hi, Fran! You look nice. Where've you been?"

"Just for a walk," I said.

"Great. That's great. Listen," she said, and she lowered her voice. "Robert's doing his three-course Italian dinner thing tonight. He wanted us all to have a meal together."

"I'd love to, Auntie Lizzie, but—"

"It would mean a lot to him. And to me, actually. We feel like we've hardly seen you. Don't you think it would be nice? The four of us?"

I didn't want to raise suspicion, and I certainly didn't want to get into a fight. Not now. I nodded. "Sure. Sounds great."

I was already calculating how early I could get out of the house.

I spent the afternoon in my room, thinking about Helen Rossdale. We didn't sit down to dinner until eight p.m., and I started to panic. I checked my phone every five minutes, and I ate the mozzarella salad and the ravioli in about three bites.

"Goodness," said Auntie Lizzie. "You're eating rather fast, Frances."

"Oh, it's just, er—it's so tasty, that's all," I said, looking at Uncle Robert. "I can't stop myself."

"You'd enjoy it even more if you actually chewed, ha-ha," said Uncle Robert. Nobody else laughed. I certainly didn't. Max stared at his food. I had ruined the atmosphere, but I couldn't help it. The clock was ticking.

My phone went. A message from Peter: *Leaving now.* I began to type an answer, but Auntie Lizzie frowned and I put the phone in my pocket. I wondered if Peter would wait for me or go straight to Vine Alley to intercept Helen. I felt like I had to be there or it would all fall apart. I imagined the four youths, filling the width of the alley.

Uncle Robert went to the kitchen and came back with some ice cream. "Neapolitan," Max said. "Nice."

"It is *not* Neapolitan," Uncle Robert said. He pointed at the ice cream, which was split into three sections: red, white, and green. "It's *spumoni*, authentic Sicilian ice cream. The green is pistachio. The colors of the Italian flag, see?"

I had to get out of the house. "Listen," I said, standing up. "This was great. Really. But I've got to go. I'll see you all later."

"Frances," said Auntie Lizzie apologetically, "do you mind telling us where you're going, love?"

"Just out. Seafront, probably."

She started to speak again but stopped. Uncle Robert put his hand on hers and took over. "We wondered if you were going to meet the, er . . . the *man* I saw you with the other day."

I sighed. "I'm not being funny, Uncle Robert, but that's my business."

"That's true to a certain extent," he said, nodding patiently. "But obviously while you're staying with us . . ."

"We don't want to be overbearing, Frances," said Auntie Lizzie.

"Don't be, then," I said. "Look, I've got to go. Can we talk about this later?"

They looked at each other. Auntie Lizzie rubbed her eyes under her glasses. "There's a lot going on in your life at the moment," she said. "Everything back home . . . We just . . . We care about you — that's all."

I nodded. "I know," I said. And I was gone.

I was later than planned, but I still had time. I knew Vine Alley was several blocks back from the beach, but the streets around there seemed to wind in tight circles. All the houses looked the same. White and regular, like teeth. I stood outside a pub, the Anchor, which was heaving with men, all facing the TV screens. I checked the map on my phone. The GPS wasn't working. I was still pretty confident that I could find the place, though.

I kept walking, quickening my pace. I took one turn, then another. The name of the streets looked familiar, but I couldn't focus. My brain was too full. I tried to call Peter, but he didn't pick up. I closed my eyes and visualized the map we had looked at earlier, but the streets had morphed into one another and reversed themselves. "Think, dammit!" I said out loud. Time was slipping away. I ran to the end of the road I was on, took a left, and felt sure I was now on the right track. Then I saw the Anchor again, and my blood turned cold. I ran back the way I'd come.

As I was running, a huge noise rose up over Helmstown, and it took me a moment to realize that people were watching the football match. It sounded like a scream of terror. A young boy in a red T-shirt emerged from a front door to my right and punched the air. "Yes! Come on, England!" he said.

His mother came out of the darkness of the house. "Leo! Back inside."

"Excuse me!" I shouted.

The mother raised her head. I saw, from her expression, how crazy I must have looked.

"I'm trying to find Vine Alley," I said.

She pointed. "That way."

I turned in the direction she'd indicated and saw Helen up ahead in the distance. I called, but she didn't hear me. I ran.

By the time the grid of Helmstown streets opened up to me, it was too late. Helen was walking quickly toward the alley. I kept sprinting, but I knew I wouldn't get there before her.

Peter came into view from the other direction, just as Helen was about to enter the alley. He called to her, and there was a brief conversation, which I couldn't hear. Peter was pointing wildly, and Helen was stepping away from him, shaking her head.

As I got closer, Peter grabbed Helen's arm, and she wrenched it away and slapped his face. Then she ran — thankfully avoiding the alley — around the corner to a parallel street.

I got to Peter a few seconds later. He was bent over slightly, holding his face. "You OK?" I said.

He took his hand away to reveal a large red palm mark.

"Well," I said, "you did it, Pete. You saved her."

"Some thanks I get," he said.

We looked down the alley and saw the gang of youths, in silhouette in the light of the streetlamp. I shuddered. "Let's get out of here," I said.

We walked back toward the beach, and my heartbeat gradually returned to normal. Stopping at the railings above the seawall, I laughed, a bit giddy with the power of changing the future. I clasped my hands together, knelt down, and pretended to pray. "Dear Lord, thank you for giving Helen . . .

what was her name again?"

"Rossdale," said Peter.

"Thanks for giving Helen Rossdale another chance. Please watch over her and make sure she uses her life well."

"And make sure she doesn't take shortcuts down dark alleys," said Peter.

"Yes! Tell her to keep to well-lit walkways."

I opened my eyes and looked at Peter, who was frowning down at the sea. "What's up, Pete?" I said.

"It wasn't God that saved her, though, was it? It wasn't about higher powers or an inevitable order. It was us. *We* did it, didn't we?"

I nodded and then so did he. I thought that maybe I was making some progress, but then a disturbing thought seemed to pierce Peter very suddenly, and he raised his hands to cover his face. "Peter? You OK?"

He didn't answer for a moment.

"Peter?" I said again.

"Do you know how long I've been a messenger?" he said.

"No."

"Years, Frances, *years*. I have lost count of the recipients. I have lost count of the people I have painted and delivered to. The people I've killed."

"But, Peter —"

"I could have saved them. All of them. Most of them, anyway. But I didn't. Oh, God," he said.

He coughed, dry retching. I went toward him. Being a messenger had given him this worldliness, an acceptance of death that made him seem older than his years, but at times like this I realized that being in your twenties wasn't that different to being a teenager. You didn't suddenly have all of life's answers. In fact, all that happened was that you'd failed a few more tests.

"Come on, Pete. It's hard, but there's nothing you can do about that now. Besides, you weren't to know."

"Why didn't Tabby tell me? Why didn't she know? I always used to feel so guilty. I always used to feel like I was *creating* the death scenes from my own imagination, you know what I mean?"

I nodded, because, strange as it sounds, I did know. For how could I draw something that wasn't somehow in my mind? And as Pablo Picasso said, *Everything you can imagine is real.*

Pete kept talking. "I used to feel that I was causing these deaths. But Tabby talked me out of it. Why?"

"She was probably trying to protect you. Just the way you tried to protect me. You always said that things couldn't be changed, and that I was just delivering the message. It was to make me feel better. It's the only thing you can do when things are out of control: try to protect your feelings."

Peter shook his head. "It's a lot of people, Frances. A lot of people gone and for nothing."

"All the more reason to make the future better than the past, Pete," I said.

I left him to it then, because I knew that what he was dealing with couldn't be cured by a few kind words and a pat on the back.

SEVENTEEN

This is the good bit of my story. The bit where everything goes right. It's a short section.

We had saved Helen Rossdale on the Monday, and on Tuesday, I met Joseph Davies, Peter's son. I'd found him on Facebook, where he called himself Joe, and there was a load of stuff on his profile about a place called Saint Paul's Rec Centre in Hartsleigh. From his picture, I could see what Peter's hair probably looked like when he was younger: light and curly and boyish.

A quick bus trip down the coast and I was there. Hartsleigh was no Helmstown. It wasn't exactly run-down, but it was very ordinary. No big white houses by the seafront or neon-lit bars or amusement arcades. Even the grass looked dull. I waited on the wall of the rec, watching the older skater boys messing around on the kids' playground, jumping off the roundabout and grinding on the benches.

It wasn't long before I noticed that I wasn't the only person watching. Joe was standing about ten meters away, just behind the Scout hut, with his own skateboard, occasionally trying a few tricks, but mainly just watching the others from a safe distance. It made me smile, watching him. I guess he'd just gone up to secondary school and he was trying to pull off a style that was a bit beyond him. He wore headphones around his neck (I could see the lead dangling aimlessly out from under his T-shirt, not plugged in), and although he was trying to wear his jeans down on his hips, he was so slim they kept falling, so that he had to catch them and drag them back up.

Again, it struck me how old the kid was, and how young Peter was when he was born. If Peter had been scared by the situation, imagine how Rowenna must have felt, bringing him up on her own.

I walked over to him. "All right?" I said.

He nodded, slightly suspicious about why a girl my age might want to talk to him. "They're pretty good, aren't they?" I said.

"Who?" he said, pretending he hadn't been staring at the other skateboarders for the last half hour.

I laughed a bit. "Those kids on the playground."

"I suppose," he said, letting his board fall to the ground.

"Do you come and watch them a lot?" I asked.

"I wasn't watching them."

"But that's how you get better, isn't it?"

He shrugged. I turned back to watch the skateboarders, but out of the corner of my eye, I saw him look me up and down.

One of the older lads tried something complicated that didn't quite come off, and his board rolled toward us. Joe stepped away, but I nodded to the lad. "Hey," he said.

"Hey," I said.

The lad walked away.

"You see," I said to Joe. "They don't bite, those guys. They're just a bit shy."

"Shy? As if! They're in year eleven."

"So?"

"Well," he said, looking longingly at them, "I wouldn't be shy if I was like them."

"But you aren't shy," I said.

He straightened up then. Proud. "No," he said. "No, I'm not. Not all the time."

"I mean, you're talking to *me,* aren't you?" I said. "A total stranger."

He nodded slowly. "You're not from round here, are you?" he said, his confidence growing.

"No. But I'm staying in Helmstown for a while. Do you know Helmstown?"

"Yeah, I've been there a couple of times," he said. Not that I believed him. "It's pretty cool."

"You been to the skate park?"

"No. I've been thinking about going. I mean, I've heard of it. I heard it's good."

"It's *beyond* good," I said. I leaned toward him and whispered, smelling the chocolate on his breath and too much deodorant. "I mean, these guys are *OK,* but the guys at Helmstown . . . Do you like stunt bikes?"

"Yes," he said.

"The stunt bike guys at Helmstown . . . *unbelievable*," I said, shaking my head as if they were something disgraceful.

Joe sighed. "Unbelievable," he said quietly.

"You should come and see them sometime," I said. "I could introduce you to some people."

"Me?" he said.

"Sure. I've been watching you. You've got . . . potential."

"I'm just . . . I'm starting out, really. I mean, it's all natural. I've taught myself. But I don't think I'm ready for the skate park yet."

"Well, you could just watch them, then, I suppose."

"I could just watch," he said.

He looked at me sideways, and he couldn't stop himself from smiling.

On my way home, I got a text from Peter: *I need to see you.*

I know that he meant we had messenger work to do, but I liked the thought that he needed me.

Peter had come straight from a plastering job on a house that was being completely renovated, and he was covered in white dust. In the dark hut, he almost glowed as he put the postcard into the scanner. "I did it this morning," he said. "Blacked out in the bathroom."

The light spilled out from under the scanner hood and moved in a bar across Peter's hands. The image came up on the screen of the laptop.

"It's one of the hardest messages I've ever done," Peter said. "So tough to find the clues."

The man was lying on the pavement, his head turned away, his hand on his stomach. Behind him was a door with no number. There was something not quite right about the picture.

"Do you know who it is?" Frances said.

"I think so," he said. "The shirt sticking out from under his sweater is the uniform of South-Eastern Trains. I went to the station after I'd done the painting, and I recognized the ticket inspector. He goes to the same supermarket as me. If I'm right, that's the door to his house. His name is Charles."

"But you can't tell how he died?"

"My best guess would be a heart attack."

"What can we do about that?" I asked.

"Unless you can turn back time and stop him from eating about twelve thousand bacon sandwiches, not a lot," Peter said. "This is the problem with your idea, Frances. And this has been my point all along: people die. It's natural."

"Don't start that again," I said. "Move over."

I zoomed in on the corner of the painting. There was a rounded piece of wood just in shot. "There. What's that?" I said.

Peter squinted. "Could be anything. . . ."

But I could tell I'd sparked his interest. "Go back to his hands," he said.

I scrolled across the painting until I came to the man's fingers resting heavily just below his chest.

"They're pretty hairy," I said.

"That's not hair. Can you zoom in any more?"

I did. We were almost down to individual brushstrokes. The shadowy marks I had taken for hairs were in fact green and black streaks. Peter smiled.

"What is it?" I asked.

"Leaf mulch and moss."

"What does it mean?"

He scrolled back to the piece of wood. "That's a ladder," he said. "He was cleaning out his roof gutter."

"He fell?"

Peter zoomed out. "Look at the angle of his neck."

Now I knew what was not quite right with the picture.

"Christ," I said.

Peter picked up some flyers for a comedy night and slipped the postcard into the pile. He went out to deliver the message and see what he could find out about Charles the ticket inspector, and I went home and made friends with Joe Davies on Facebook. I sent him some videos of kids doing stunts on the half-pipes of Helmstown beach.

I was taking control of things, and it felt good.

EIGHTEEN

Two days later, I sneaked out of the house at dawn and met up with Peter. We set off for Charles Gregan's house (Peter had found out his surname) to steal his faulty ladder. Like the day before, it was windy.

I could see how Peter's decision to try to save his recipients was already changing him. His shoulders were straighter, stronger, and there was a new urgency about his movements. He had bought a couple of leather-bound diaries so we could organize our schedules.

"Where does he keep the ladder?" I said.

"Down the side of his house. I saw it when I delivered the message."

"Pete?" I said.

"Yes."

"What if he borrows someone else's ladder?"

"That's not our problem," Peter said. "We're changing the picture on the postcard. Maybe the weather will be better by the time he gets another ladder. Maybe he won't bother cleaning the gutter. But we can't follow him around for the rest of his life. We can only go so far."

Peter pulled up short when he saw the house from across the street.

"What's wrong?" I said, following his gaze. The gutter pipe under the roof of the house was broken and hanging down in two places. The curtains were open—the only ones open at that time of the morning. A dark patch stained the pavement outside the front door, and one of the slabs was cracked.

"Wow. He really does have to fix that gutter," I said.

"No," Peter said. "I don't like this."

"What?" I said.

"Think about the picture. The message," Peter said.

We crossed the road. Shards of wood were scattered on the concrete. The stain on the pavement contained bright-green moss, leaves, dirt, and a darker, brownish substance which had seeped into the fracture in the slab.

"I don't understand," I said. "What's going on?"

Peter shook his head and moved quickly down the side of the house. He came back out a few seconds later. "No ladder," he said. "Something has gone wrong. It looks like it's already . . . It can't be."

"Are you sure you got the right day?"

"Of course I did!" he shouted.

I looked down.

"I'm sorry," he said.

"What are we going to do?" I said.

"I don't know," he said. "I need to think."

He began to walk away. I waited for a moment, and because I did, I was able to hear a woman inside the house, sobbing. I shivered and hurried after Peter.

It was then I found the ladder. Half of it, anyway. It was in a skip down the road. "Peter!" I shouted, and he came back.

I took hold of the jagged end, where it had snapped.

"Rotten," he said.

"Maybe it's not the same ladder."

"We'll soon find out."

He went into the newsagent's. I heard him having a conversation with the man at the till. Then he came out and started walking toward the beach.

"What did he say?" I said.

"It has already happened. He said that a man fell off his ladder yesterday morning. He broke his neck and died in hospital."

"But I don't understand. That's a day early."

"Yes," Peter said. "Yes, it is. Twenty-four hours after I drew him. That's never happened before."

We went to the Coffee Shack. I had to order because of Peter's incident with Helen outside Vine Alley. Peter sat at one of the metal tables looking out onto the sea. I put our drinks down and sat next to him. I was shaken up.

"What's happening?" I said.

He didn't answer for a while. Then he looked at me. "I don't know. Something Tabby said . . . Death adapts," he said. His face was blank. "It evolves, just as we do, only quicker. It has the whole world, and everything in it, to use as tools."

He'd gone back to his old self, and I could see why. There was a randomness to being a messenger. Sometimes it was like we were thrashing around in the dark. But I wouldn't give up.

"We meddled with the process," Peter said. "We tried to change the future. We lost."

"So we'll fight back. If it's twenty-four hours, we'll work faster."

"It will adapt again."

"Well, then so will we!" I said. "We can't just quit, Peter. There's too much at stake."

"We're not in control of it. I told you there'd be consequences," he said.

"And I told *you* there'd be consequences. One of which was that you might be able to see your son. Either you want to do that or you don't." I winced with pain.

"What's wrong?" he said.

"Splinter. From that stupid ladder."

"Let me see."

It had dug into the pad of flesh under my thumb. Peter held my hand and looked. "Got any tweezers?" he said.

"Do I look like the sort of girl who carries tweezers?" I said.

He brought my hand to his mouth. I sort of froze, feeling his lips against my skin, and a little bit of pain as his teeth searched for the splinter. He bit down, pulled it free, then gave me back my hand. The spit cooled.

We were both quiet for a moment.

"I never said I was quitting," he said.

When we saw the van pull up by the newsagent's and drop off the morning edition of the local newspaper, I went across to get a copy and confirm what we already suspected. I remember seeing the picture of Charles Gregan on page two, and I remember crossing the road toward Peter, but after that, it was all a blur.

I came back to full consciousness on the floor of Peter's hut. He was stroking my hair. I closed my eyes for a moment and let him think I was still out of it, hoping he'd carry on. With his hands on me like that, I could pretend that we'd just woken up together.

"You OK?" he said, probably seeing my eyelids flutter.

"It never stops, does it?" I said.

"No," he said, handing me the new postcard. A young boy on the floor of a café. For a moment I was petrified that it might be Joe Davies. But it wasn't. This boy was much younger.

"Any clues?" I said.

"No," Peter said. "It seems to be getting harder."

"And now we've only got one day," I said.

"I suppose we have to assume that's the case. Look," he said. "You're tired. Why don't you go home, and I'll work on this? I owe you one, for the girl on her hen night."

When I got back to Auntie Lizzie's, Joe Davies had left a message for me on Facebook, a response to the skater videos I'd sent. The message was just one word:

Unbelievable.

NINETEEN

The boy was about eight years old and wearing a bright-red T-shirt. He was drinking his apple juice on the table next to us, in a café that backed onto a small park on the outskirts of Helmstown. Peter and I were nervous, casting sly glances at him and his mother. We'd put the postcard on his table and pretended to be handing out flyers. One day wasn't much time, and we'd cut it fine.

"It's probably the apple juice that attracts the wasp," Peter whispered, tightening his rolled-up newspaper. Peter had spent ages zooming in on my postcard and had eventually noticed a swelling on the boy's neck. Using a medical textbook, he'd identified the swelling as a massive reaction to a wasp sting. Anaphylactic shock. I never would have discovered it.

After saving his first recipient, Peter had started reading books on philosophy. He had one on the table now. *Knowledge and Reality: Essays in Honor of Alvin Plantinga.* He kept going on about all the possible futures, which was a nice change from before, when he thought there was just one gloomy future.

The boy was sullen and irritable. "What's this rubbish?" he said, picking up the postcard. He was one of those Helmstown kids who looks like he has a personal stylist. If his trousers were too short, it was because they were *meant* to be like that.

"Eat your sandwich, Leo," his mother said.

"I don't want it," he said.

"Come on, love. It's serrano ham, your favorite."

He tutted.

"Why can't we just drag him out of here now?" I said. "I mean, theoretically, any little change we make will stop the wasp from stinging him, won't it? Even if we knock his sandwich over or ask him to move chairs . . ."

"Not necessarily," Peter said, opening his philosophy book. "If we accept that there are infinite possible futures, we don't know in how many of those futures the wasp stings the boy. If we call the future that the postcard predicts X—"

"Peter."

"What?"

"If you see the wasp, hit it."

There was a song on the café radio with a guitar line full of buzzes, and Peter and I got jittery. Fortunately we saw the wasp fly in through the window and land on the table by Leo's sandwich.

Peter stepped across to the table and brought the rolled-up newspaper down. Leo's mother flinched in shock, and Leo cried out. The wasp was only wounded and made its angry way toward the boy. I swooped in and smashed the very heavy hardback of *Knowledge and Reality* down on the insect. I lifted up the book and swept the crushed body off the table. "Nasty little things," I said.

"Thank you," said Leo's mother eventually. "Leo's allergic to wasps, aren't you, love?"

Leo's face was thunder. "No need to broadcast it!" he said.

Peter smiled at him and then turned to me. "You couldn't save the wasp?" he said quietly.

Peter binned the insect, and we walked out of the café. When we had got far enough away, we started running and shouting with triumph. "We did it! We did it!" Peter said.

"We're saving the world!" I said.

Peter stopped suddenly and looked off into the distance, thinking. I stood beside him. We were both breathing hard, and that was the loudest sound, with the shouting of kids in the distance. I put my head on his shoulder. He stiffened, as though I was making him uncomfortable, and I raised my head quickly, looking away.

We walked back through the park. Plenty of little kids were enjoying the hot weather, and Peter and I tried not to see the danger in the girls climbing trees, or the boys trying to fish a tennis ball out of the pond, or the homeless guy drinking too much white cider, or the woman crossing the busy T-junction.

Near the swings, we saw Leo with a group of friends. "It's an amazing feeling, isn't it?" I said.

"What?" Peter said.

"That boy. Leo. If it wasn't for us, he wouldn't be playing out here in the sun. He'd be on his way to the hospital."

"Hmm," Peter said.

"It gives you hope, doesn't it?" I said as we got nearer to the group of kids. "It gives you the feeling that you could really *do* something in this world."

It became clear that Leo and his friends were in a circle around a large boy who wore a baggy T-shirt over his big belly.

"Show us your boobs, fatty," one of the boys said.

"Yeah, come on, you fat pig," said Leo.

I looked into the eyes of the large boy. The pain there told me this was not his first time in the middle of a circle. He looked desperate. I was outraged. I'm not a fan of bullying at the best of times, and now I felt betrayed by the boy we'd saved.

"Hey!" I said, grabbing Leo and pulling him aside. "What do you think you're doing?"

"None of your business," he said.

"Yes, it bloody is," I said. "You leave that boy alone."

"You better leave me alone. If you don't, I'll call my mum, who's a personal assistant for a politician, and you'll be in a whole world of trouble."

"Don't threaten me, you little —"

I felt a hand on my shoulder. It was Peter, dragging me away. The large boy had managed to escape and was running for the playground.

"Let's leave it now, shall we?" said Peter, nodding at a group of parents who had come into view. We walked away, although

I cast a look back at Leo. "I'll be watching you," I said to him.

"Witch," he said.

When we got back to the beach hut, Peter was shaking his head. "What?" I said, taking my sketch pad and pencil tin out of my rucksack.

"You see?" he said. "Consequences. You save a boy, and he goes outside and bullies another kid. Are you going to follow Leo around, saving all the poor children whose lives he ruins?"

I sighed. "Look, Leo might be a nasty spoiled brat now, but human beings can change. They can get better."

"All I'm saying is that when you interfere with the way things are, you set off a chain of new events. Not all of them are good."

"Well, I reckon there'll be more good results than bad."

"I'm not so sure."

"Peter. I've got something to tell you." I paused. "I met Joseph."

I was expecting another outburst, but he was so controlled in that moment. I thought I'd got away with it.

But then he took my tin and he started snapping my Berol Venus pencils as he spoke. "You. Do. Not. Think. Do you? You do not listen."

"I'm trying to help," I said, trying to hold it together while the pencil pieces fell to the floor.

"You're trying to ruin my life," he said. *Snap. Snap. Snap.*

"Don't be such a drama queen, Peter."

"Oh, I'm being dramatic, am I? Worrying about my only son? Point one: I've not been working on saving recipients for long enough to be sure I can do it every time. We don't know the consequences of what we're doing. Point two: The rules—in case you hadn't noticed—keep changing. Point three: *Your* drawing is not good enough yet. Mine is, but yours isn't. You could draw him and the image might be too rough to work out where he is. Have you considered that?"

He dropped the last of the broken pencils to the floor. There was a slight smell of cedar in the air. Smoky and rich. "I think I *am* good enough," I said quietly.

"Great!" he said. "That's just great. I admire your confidence. Let's test it out on the only person in the world that matters to me."

I was hurt by that.

"Well, *you* don't matter to *him*," I said.

"What do you mean?"

"He doesn't even know you."

Peter stood up, breathing heavily. Particles of dust drifted from his fingers. My heart thumped in the silence.

"He's a bit like you," I said.

"I don't want to know about . . . Peter trailed off, because he *did* want to know. Of course he did.

"He's clever. He's got goodness in him," I said.

Peter rubbed his face. "Must get that from his mother."

"No. Not just his mother. He gets it from you, too."

"Well, like you say, he's never even met me," Peter said.

"And if he did, his life would be better," I said.

"What's wrong with his life?" Peter said.

"Nothing much. But it would be better with you in it. I know you don't believe that, but trust me — it's true."

"Look, just because you don't know your dad, Frances, doesn't mean he's a good person."

"I'm not talking about *my* dad. I'm talking about you. You'd be good for him, not just because you're his dad but because of who you are."

"Oh, come on. I'm a —"

"No!" I said. "You're a good man. You're someone who wants to do the right thing. And you care about people. You might not bloody show it much, but you do."

Peter shook his head.

"Anyway, he's coming to Helmstown on Saturday," I said.

"Jesus, Frances."

"He's coming to watch the skaters. About three p.m."

"It's too soon. There's absolutely no way I'm going to be there. And if you've got any sense at all, you'll stay away, too."

"I can't let him down," I said.

That sentence, and everything it might mean, tumbled around the hut. Peter walked out, leaving a cloud of dust and ten broken pencils behind him.

What was I doing? Why would I go through so much for this man? At the time, I didn't really have a chance to reflect on what I was feeling for Peter. What did I know about love? Most of the crushes I'd had on boys at school had more to do with fitting in. They were just friendships, really — perfectly nice, but nothing like this. This was physical, real. It was like weather: fierce, changeable, and I couldn't do a thing about it. I spent most of my time with Peter talking about how we had the power to control what we did and how we felt. But I was completely unable to resist this force of attraction to him. I didn't know what it was, but I knew I couldn't turn it off.

And I knew he didn't feel it about me. There was nothing I could do about that, either.

TWENTY

I roped Max into coming with me to meet Joe, and we waited for him in town on a rare bright day. With the sea looming in the background, Joe looked even younger as he came toward us, holding his skateboard in front of his chest like a shield.

"Hi, Joe," I said. "This is my cousin, Max."

"Hey," Max said.

Joe nodded, but then spoke quietly to me. "I thought it was just going to be you," he said.

"Max is cool. You don't have to worry. He's well known at the skate park."

"Right," Joe said. "I'm not bothered or anything. It's just that I like to know what's going on."

I could tell, for all his bravado, that he was nervous, that coming to Helmstown was a big deal for him. As we walked toward the beach, I tried to make small talk and put him at ease.

"Did you get a lift here?"

"No," he said. "I just jumped on the bus. It was easy."

"Right," I said.

"But my mum knows where I am," he added quickly. I could see that was probably a lie.

"I'm not going to kidnap you," I said with a smile.

"Well . . . you *couldn't*," he said indignantly. "Anyway, I don't know if I'll hang around for long, because I've got lots of mates in Helmstown and I should really hook up with them."

Another lie. Max gave me a little alarmed look, as if to say, "Who is this kid, and what are we doing?"

Joe started to relax as soon as he saw the skate park. The floodlights, loaded with trainers, were the first things that came into view. The kids had chucked their old shoes up there, with the laces tied together. Knackered Vans and Adidas hung off the lights, like catkins from tree branches. I could tell that Joe was already lost to the legend of the place. Pretty soon we could see the stunt bikers looping up above the path, big and unreal against the blue screen of the sea and sky.

"Jesus," Joe said in a hushed voice as we went down the steps to beach level.

The skate park was set back from the beach and had two quarter-pipes and a ramp in the middle with rails. Groups of kids stood at the top of the quarter-pipes, waiting, watching, laughing. There were two or three kids there who were incredibly good. A guy on a stunt bike who could go head over heels and spin the handlebars in the air. All that stuff.

Joe looked up at them with such awe that I thought he might fall over backward.

"You coming in?" Max said to Joe.

"Nah," said Joe, trying to act nonchalant. "I think I might watch for a bit."

Max took his board over and bumped fists with a few of the other boys, did some tricks. He looked like he knew what he was doing.

"Your cousin is *amazing*," Joe said.

"Yeah," I said.

"This whole place . . ." he said, looking out over the beach scene, the girls with knots in their T-shirts, the volleyball players in the sandpit, the day-trip drinkers, the reggae band outside the beach bar, the man making chalk drawings.

"Helmstown? Good, isn't it?"

Another little suspicious glance broke through, but before he could ask why I was being so nice, I spoke up. "Hey, let's go around the other side and get a better view."

We strolled over, the rumble of wheels occasionally broken by the silence of someone leaving the ground. We stood near the man who was chalking a picture on the black tarmac. It was stunning. A blazing, fiery sun in orange and red, with a guy on a skateboard suspended in front of it. The guy on the board was left blank, so the tarmac made him look like a shadow across the sun. It was so good that for a moment I was distracted from the nagging sense that I recognized the style.

Then I looked at the artist, hunched over his work.

He was wearing a baseball cap and dark glasses.

Peter.

I turned to look at Joe, but he wasn't there. A few not very pleasant thoughts passed through my mind until I realized he was standing behind me. He took a step toward Peter. A step toward his dad. And he stared at the chalk.

"What do you think?" I said.

Peter stopped drawing and waited for the answer.

"Awesome," Joe whispered.

"Awesome," I said, loud enough so that Peter could hear.

Peter took a deep breath. I could see his hand shaking, the red dust picking out the pattern of calluses on his skin. "Do you think so?" he said. He didn't dare look up.

"Yeah," said Joe. "The way you've done the thing with the figure, leaving him blank."

I watched the rounded ends of Joe's trainers shuffle toward the giant sun.

"Thank you," Peter said. His voice was quivering, and it seemed like a strange scene to me: this strong man kneeling on the pavement, unable to make eye contact with a young boy. "You sound like an expert."

"Not really," Joe said with a shrug. "You know, I like art, but not the way they teach it at school."

Peter smiled broadly. I wondered what he could hear in the boy's voice. Whether he could hear Rowenna's accent. "What's your name?" Peter said.

"Joseph. My mates call me Joe."

"Can I call you Joe?" Peter said.

"Sure," Joe said, sounding quite pleased.

Peter placed the small piece of red chalk on the ground, next to the image. He took a while to make up his mind, to fight off his fears, but eventually he did it.

He looked up.

I could tell Peter was close to tears. His mouth was open and dry. He managed to smile, and Joe, who had no idea of the meaning of the moment, smiled back.

"What's *your* name?" Joe said.

"It's . . . it's Paul," Peter said.

"Cool," Joe said.

Max came over. "All right?" he said to me. He didn't notice Peter and instead turned to Joe. "So, like, are you going to come in or what?" he said, pointing to the skate park.

"Oh. I mean I've not really . . ." Joe said. I'd never seen someone want to do something so much in my life.

"You're not going to get better standing there," Max said. "Come on. You can meet some of the others."

He gestured to the boys at the top of the quarter-pipe, and they raised their heads and nodded.

Joe looked at me and I shrugged.

"I guess," said Joe. He was trying not to smile, but he was failing miserably. He took a big breath of salty air and followed Max up to the quarter-pipe, where he struggled through a couple of complicated handshakes.

I waited a few moments and then turned to Peter. He was in a heap, the breeze pulling little wisps of colored dust off the chalk. He looked at me, and for a moment I was convinced he would shatter into a thousand pieces. The world is too much for some people.

"You OK, Pete?" I asked.

"I think, for the first time in a long while, the answer to that question might be yes."

He took his sunglasses off and looked at me. His eyes were red and swollen, but they were full of something like relief. I took a bottle of water out of my bag and gave it to him. He put it to his lips and drank.

"So," I said, "this could be the start of something."

"I don't know," Peter said.

"But we managed to save those people and—"

"It's too early, Frances. What about Charles Gregan? We don't know what will happen next."

"Nobody does, Pete. That's life. But you can take it slow."

"He's a good boy," Peter said. "At least I know that. So much of his mother about him."

We turned to watch Joe coming down the pipe, his eyes wide and his T-shirt rippling. To me, people on skateboards always look strange, because they're standing sideways. As if they're trying to move without you noticing. As if they're jumping the queue. But there was something quite graceful about Joe. "He's not bad," I said.

Peter laughed, but he couldn't quite reply. He lit a cigarette instead and rubbed his eyes.

The sun became clouded. Only Peter's chalk sun still burned bright. The stunt bikers were like silvery fish coming off the ramps, and the rumble of wheels went on and on.

Joe was coming down at quite a pace, his confidence

growing with the encouragement from Maxi and his friends. But then he tried the rail and slipped. His ankle buckled, and he hit the ground.

He tried to stand up and be brave, but he collapsed again as soon as he put his weight down.

"Shit," I said.

Peter and I ran over to him and nudged through the crowd. Peter put his hands out toward his boy, but then took them back, as if he might turn Joe to stone if he touched him.

"Are you OK, Joe?" I said.

He whispered so quietly, I could barely hear him. "No," he said, and I could see that he was no longer pretending that he wasn't an eleven-year-old. I could also see that the ankle had swollen badly already. I looked daggers at Max, who shrugged. "Shall we call an ambulance?" he said.

"No," said Joe. "I'll be fine. It's probably just sprained."

"Call a taxi," I told Max.

"Where we going?" Max said.

"Joe and I are going to the ER," I said.

"You need help getting him up the steps?" Max said, pointing back to the seawall.

"I'll do it," Peter said.

I looked at him. "Right," I said. "Let's get him lifted."

Peter and I took hold of Joe by the shoulders and helped him onto one leg. The three of us struggled up the steps, Peter with his son's skateboard under his free arm.

"We're going to need some help on the other side," I said to Peter as we waited for the taxi.

Peter nodded.

When the car came, we carefully slid into the back and I put Joe's leg over my knees.

He smiled weakly and took out his phone. "I have to call my mum."

I looked at Peter, but he just closed his eyes. I suddenly felt a sense of regret, as though I'd made everything move too fast. Things were getting out of control.

TWENTY-ONE

A cloudy dusk came on quickly. Other lights shone: the locked-door lights in the taxi, Joe's luminous watch, the orange street-light sliding over Peter's face as he looked at his son. The hospital was boiling hot, and the sickly strip lighting picked out every gash on the early Saturday boozers. Day-trippers whose day trips were slipping into a bad place. Like Joe's.

We signed in at the desk, and I sat in a seat across from Joe and held his foot up on my thigh. "You're supposed to do rest, ice, compression, and elevation," I said.

"Thanks," he said.

Peter paced up and down, looking for staff to harass. He couldn't cope with seeing Joe in pain.

Eventually he sat down on the rubbery seat next to his son. It made a rip-roaring fart noise. Joe held his serious, mature face for about two seconds, but then he couldn't help himself. He laughed. It was a good, infectious laugh, and I caved, too. Then Peter did. He stood up and sat down again, and the noise was the same. He turned to the miserable old guy sitting on the other side of him who was holding his wrist, and he said, "I'm in for gas — what are you in for?"

Joe totally cracked up then. The nice thing about his laugh was that he had tried to resist it. It made him helpless. Within a few seconds, a good percentage of the people sitting there were laughing along with him, even if they didn't know what the joke was. I could have sworn I even saw a smile on the face of the old fella with the dodgy wrist.

I had my back to the door, so I didn't know why Peter and Joe stopped laughing so suddenly. I figured there were only a couple of options — either some poor guy had walked in carrying his own head or Joe's mother had arrived.

I looked over my shoulder. She had a kind face, and she'd dyed two blond streaks into the front of the black hair that Peter had written about in the letter. She bit her lip and scanned the waiting area.

I looked back at Joe and Peter. Joe, who still had his foot on my knee, waved at his mother, and Peter looked down at his hands, which he'd folded on his stomach, as if he were trying to stop the blood coming out of a bullet hole.

"Mum!" Joe shouted.

"Oh, Joseph!" she said. Her flip-flops slapped the floor. She came toward us, but she only had eyes for her boy.

"Honey, are you OK?"

"Yes, Mum. I fell on my ankle at the skate park — that's all."

"What were you even doing there?" she said. She didn't sound angry, just confused.

"I was . . . nothing. I was on my skateboard. Frances and Paul brought me in," he said.

"Thank you," Rowenna said to me distractedly.

I couldn't speak. I could barely even nod, because I knew what was coming.

She looked up at Peter, and the word *thanks* got sliced in midair. Her eyes widened, and she took a big step back. Her hand went up to her mouth. "Peter," she said. She said it with love, but that might have been accidental.

I knew it wouldn't last, anyway.

I kept my eyes on Joe. Looking at anyone else was pretty much unbearable. But I was interested, too. I wanted to see what it was like to recognize your dad for the first time. He couldn't quite take it in. "You said your name was Paul," he said.

I suppose he had an image in his head of his father. A cross between various film characters and the stories his mum had told him. Just the way Johnny had given me an image of our dad. But now he was faced with the truth. He looked between Rowenna and Peter. "Mum?" he said.

She dropped her car keys, and the noise of them hitting the floor seemed to shake Peter to life.

"I'll leave," he said. He still didn't look up. He just stared at his cupped hands. Then he stood. "He needs treatment. I just wanted to make sure he was OK."

Rowenna made a strange gasp, almost a laugh. "You wanted *to make sure he was OK*?" she said. "Peter, where the hell have you been?" She looked him over. "What *happened* to you? Why didn't you . . . ? Oh, Jesus."

She began to cry. She tried to apologize to Joe, but she couldn't get the words out. The atmosphere and the confusion (and probably the pain) had got to Joe, too, and he was also tearing up. He put his hand on his mum's arm.

Peter didn't look at me. He didn't look at anyone. He just turned around and started walking down the corridor.

"What, you're just going to . . . ?" Rowenna said, but he didn't hear.

It had all gone wrong, and there wasn't much doubt whose fault it was.

TWENTY-TWO

I just sat there.

Joe had eased himself back down and his mum was next to him, where Peter had been sitting. It was obvious that there would be questions and strong words later, but now they were just holding on to each other. It was weird, and comforting — even to me.

A nurse with a clipboard came. "Joseph Davies?" she said.

They both stood up.

"I want to go in on my own," Joe said. "I'm old enough."

"I don't think that's a good idea. I think you've been doing a bit too much on your own today."

"Mum, please. I can manage."

Rowenna could see that he was still upset.

"OK," she said. "I'll be right here."

He hobbled off, his arm around the nurse, and Rowenna slumped back down into the seat. I didn't know what else to do, so I got a plastic cup, filled it up at the water cooler, and took it to her. She looked up at me.

"Thanks," she said. "Wait. Who *are* you?"

"Frances," I said.

"Why are you here?" There was a note of anger in her voice now, which was fair enough.

"Because all of this is my fault."

"That he fell over?"

"No. It's my fault that he met Peter. I'm Peter's friend. I arranged for him to meet Joe."

Rowenna closed her eyes. "Peter should not have done that."

"It was me."

"You're just a girl."

"Still," I said. "Look, I can see I made a mistake, and I guess you're very pissed off right now. But don't be angry with Peter, because it wasn't his idea; it was mine."

"Don't tell me who I should and shouldn't be angry with! Clearly there have been a lot of things going on that I've not been aware of. I'm not very happy about that, and I certainly don't want to talk about my and my *son's* private life with some girl I've never met before," she said.

"You don't want to know about Peter?"

She paused. "Not really."

"You know he has always thought about you. And Joe."

"What? That's rubbish! If he's been thinking about us, then where the hell has he been for the last eleven years? A check in the post is not enough. And now *this*!"

A few of the injured people in the waiting room looked over at us.

"He does care about you both. It's just . . ." How could I tell her about being a messenger? "You have to trust me."

"Trust you? I don't even know who you are! I'm not going to sit here and listen to a teenager explain my bloody life to me. If Peter wants to tell me about where he's been, then he has to be brave enough to stand here and say it himself."

"You're saying you'd talk to him?" I said. "If he was here?"

"No!" she said. Then she looked down into her cup and shook her head. "I don't know. Yes. I just want to know what happened. But he walked out again, didn't he? Just like last time."

All of a sudden it occurred to me that I might be able to turn this situation around. What had these past few weeks been about? Taking control. Changing things.

"Wait here," I said, standing.

"What else am I going to do?" she said.

I stepped outside and felt the coolness of the night. *A taxi*, I thought, *I'll get a taxi to the beach hut and drag him back here.* I ran toward the taxi rank, but then I stopped in my tracks. I had spotted something unusual out of the corner of my eye. Peter.

He was sitting on top of the bus shelter, smoking, his legs swinging over the edge. There was a man standing in the shelter, and either he hadn't seen Peter or was choosing to ignore him.

"Oi," I said.

He gave me a glance.

"Get down off there," I said.

"Haven't you done enough?" he said.

"She wants to talk to you," I said.

"She wants to shout at me, more like," he said.

"Well, she has every reason to, hasn't she? You've got to take hold of your life, Peter. Now's the time to do it. If you love her like you say you do, then get down off the bus shelter, get back in that building, and talk to her."

It wasn't easy for me to say that. I knew that he still had feelings for Rowenna. And even though Rowenna was angry, you don't get angry with people you don't care about.

The man waiting for the bus stared at me and then cast a look up at Peter. I could see Peter searching his brain for reasons he couldn't go back to the hospital, but it seemed he'd run out of excuses.

They sat in the hospital café and talked. Leaving them there, across a plastic table in a dim and empty little room, I saw how much Peter had changed since I first met him. His shoulders were relaxed, and he sat tall and straight.

He looked at Rowenna. For most people, looking someone in the eye is no big deal, but for Peter it was always a risk. As if he might suck the person in and then spill their life onto the page. But I was proud of Peter for taking some control over how he dealt with being a messenger. *Who knows what might happen from here?* I thought.

I intercepted Joe in the corridor. He was on crutches. "You OK?" I said.

"It's just a sprain. I'll be off these in a couple of days. Where's Mum?"

"She's just having a chat with . . . Peter."

Joe winced and turned away. It was all too much for him. He was in denial, I suppose.

"I'm sure she'll fill you in," I said.

"I'd like to see her now," he said. "And I want to go home."

So we walked around to the café entrance, Joe struggling on the crutches. At the entrance, he paused. Rowenna's eyes were wet. Peter was nodding. And he was talking. I knew it'd take more than five minutes and a couple of crap hot chocolates to rub out the last eleven years, but it was a start.

Rowenna looked up but not toward us. There was another door, and a man walked through it. He was a typical Helmstown man, like Uncle Robert—about forty-five but with a side-swinging fringe and a coat with those tags on the shoulders like they have in the army. "Ro!" shouted the guy, in his posh voice. She waved to him.

"I came as soon as I could," he said. "How's Joe?"

It was as if we weren't there. Like we were the Ghosts of Christmas Past. "Who the hell's that?" I said to Joseph.

"That's Ian," Joseph said.

On hearing Joe's voice, Ian turned and said, "Speak of the devil."

I reckon Pete and me both thought he was talking about us.

TWENTY-THREE

I got the bus back to Auntie Lizzie's. I sat upstairs, and a
drunk boy was holding his cricket hat out the window to
hear the flapping sound it made. It reminded me of running
through Nana's house with my blank piece of flapping paper,
running through the garden, and climbing over the little wire
fence into the fields. I got that wretched feeling again. Like
hell was round the corner. Looking back, I realized that I
must have drawn something that day, all those years ago. My
first proto-message. It would have been a harmless squiggle.
Indecipherable. A dud. Nonetheless, that must have been the
moment I became a messenger.

It turned out that Ian was Rowenna's partner. In the
hospital café, he had shaken hands with Peter, and his
eyebrows had twitched a little. Rowenna, I figured, would
explain things to Joe and Ian later. Maybe she was doing it right
now. Peter hadn't looked too glum when Ian called Rowenna
"darling." I suppose he'd been expecting as much. He always
imagined the worst.

I was tired by the time I got to Auntie Lizzie's, and I didn't want to talk. I intended to sneak in through the back entrance, but when I passed the open kitchen window, I heard them speak.

". . . all I'm saying is that we ought to know where she is. She's our responsibility, really," said Uncle Robert.

"You're right, I know. She *is* a good girl, though, Robert," said Auntie Lizzie.

"She's brilliant. Clever. Funny. But I don't know if she has many boundaries at home. Your sister —"

"Louise gets depressed. And after everything that's happened with Johnny . . ."

"That's what I'm saying. Frances needs some security in her life. Some attention. And at the moment, the attention she's getting is from this guy, and we don't know anything about him."

"What did he look like?"

"Tall. Sort of good-looking. From his clothes, I'd say he was a painter or laborer or something. Late twenties maybe. Too old, really."

"But what are we supposed to do? We've tried talking to her."

"Well, if *she* won't listen . . . maybe I could have a word with Brian, down at the station," Robert said. Then he stopped. "What was that noise?"

I crept back round to the front of the house, opened the door, and ran upstairs before they could speak to me.

Up in my room, I called Mum. I flicked my mobile on to

loudspeaker and chucked it on the bed, waiting for the voice mail to kick in. But, amazingly, she answered.

"Hello, Frances," she said. She sounded numb. I grabbed the phone.

"Any news about Johnny?" I asked immediately.

"No."

"Right."

We were both silent for a moment. I hadn't thought beyond questions about my brother.

"So," she said. "Everything OK down there, is it?"

"Not really."

"Oh, come on, Frances! Don't try to guilt me. You're in the lap of luxury. I know you like it better down there than you do up here. You're the lucky one. There are other people in this world with bigger problems than you, you know."

"I don't want to fight, Mum."

"Don't wind me up, then," she said.

I thought of a million smart-arse replies, but I let them all float away.

"Don't go quiet on me, Frances. Come on, what have you been up to?"

"Nothing, really. Just helping out."

"Helping out, eh?"

I could hear the accusation in her voice. Helping someone else was always seen as a failure to help her. It was disloyal. I could have reacted, but for once I didn't.

"Frances? Are you there?"

"Why did he leave us, Mum?" I said.

"Because he thinks they're going to lock him up and throw away the key," she said.

"No, not Johnny. Dad. Why did Dad leave us?"

I thought Mum might tighten up. I'd asked that question so many times before and she'd just freeze. But she breathed out slowly. Maybe she was about to start telling the truth. Perhaps she was too shattered to keep lying.

"Your father didn't leave us," she said. "We ran away. We had to. He hit me and Johnny so hard, I didn't know if we'd survive."

"What?" I said.

"The beatings were nothing compared to what he'd say to us. The cruelty of it. Johnny was only a boy. I don't know if he ever got over it, really. As soon as I saw you, darlin', the second you were born, I knew we had to go. You was so small, so fragile."

She stopped.

"Mum?"

"I shouldn't be telling you all this. I don't know why I am. Usually, I'd —"

"It's OK," I said.

She didn't speak. So I did.

"But Johnny had all these stories about Dad," I said quietly.

"You mean the ones he told you when you got home from school?"

"How did you know about that?"

"I used to listen at the door." She sighed. "Oh, Frances. He made them up. Every last one. But don't be angry with him, Fran. He was only trying to do something nice."

I wasn't angry. It was suddenly obvious that they'd been lies. Deep down, I think I'd known all the time. But was it really so wrong? There was still goodness and brilliance in those stories. It's just that the goodness and brilliance had come from Johnny, not my dad.

"I asked him about the stories once," Mum said. *"Why you telling her all them lies?'* I said. He said he just wanted you to have the dad you deserved."

I didn't cry, but it was a struggle. Mum was crying now. I could hear her. "I just want Johnny back, Frances. He's not like you. He's not a survivor."

People had always wondered why Johnny and me were so different. He was so wild, and I was all common sense. He went off the rails, while I did well at school. He took all that punishment in the boxing ring. Now it was clear to me why. He'd known our dad, and I hadn't.

"He'll be all right, Mum," I said.

"But how do you know, Frances?" she said.

She was right. I didn't.

When Mum and I hung up, I went over to the window and asked Johnny to come back. I asked him to remember the story he'd told me about how our dad had twisted the spring out of his finger. I told Johnny I knew that he'd made the story up, which meant that it was him — Johnny — who was the clever one. "You've got a good brain, Johnny," I whispered into the night. "You can do this. You can make the right decision. Come back."

But I knew he'd be thinking about jail. I knew he'd think

there was no way out of the situation. He'd be scared stiff that the policeman would die and that they'd call him a murderer. But he wasn't a murderer, was he?

I had been telling Peter to face up to his life, to take control of it, to take action. But what had I done about Johnny? Nothing. I had assumed he was a lost cause, in much the same way Peter had assumed that seeing his son was a lost cause. Sometimes it's hard to take your own advice.

The conversation with Mum had shaken me out of my negative thinking about Johnny's situation. I had changed Peter's life, so surely I could change my own. Thinking about Johnny making up those stories on my bed, I knew I had to keep trying to help him. Maybe I didn't need some stupid lawyer to find out if he had a case.

TWENTY-FOUR

I didn't consider going to anyone else. Max is a great guy, and Auntie Lizzie is very understanding, but when you're a messenger, you have a certain view of the world. You develop a way of looking into the future, of seeing how each decision you make could set off an unstoppable cascade of events. So when I was working out how I could help Johnny, I wanted to speak to someone who shared that view. I called Peter and we arranged to meet on the sea path.

He was wearing a crisp white shirt, which still had the creases from the piece of cardboard they put in the packaging. The whiteness of the collar exaggerated the toasted color of his skin. Windburn, sunburn. He looked good.

He didn't see me approaching because he was struggling with the cuffs. "You're dandy today," I said.

He looked up. "Frances!" he said. "Do you think this is too small?"

"No. Guys wear them tight."

"It's been a long time since I've thought about fashion."

That was true. He wasn't like other guys his age, but I guess he'd always had a lot on his mind.

We walked toward the hut through a stiff summer wind.

"I'm a bit nervous," he said.

"Have a cigarette. That's what you usually do."

"I've quit."

"Wow. Where are you going, anyway?"

"I'm going to Hartsleigh. Rowenna invited me. I didn't want to look scruffy."

I'll admit to it, although I don't like to: I felt more than a twinge of jealousy. There wasn't much I could do about it. After all, it was me who had got them to speak to each other again. Sometimes when you feel like you're never going to get with the person you love, when the whole situation feels impossible, you just *want* them to be with someone else. You want it to be over, so there is absolutely no chance. There's nothing more painful than a glimmer of hope.

I clenched my teeth. "Great news," I said.

"We're going to sit down for a coffee, talk everything through. Me, Rowenna, and What's-His-Name."

"Ian," I said.

"Yeah."

"So," I said. "All of a sudden you're the sort of man who *sits down for coffee*. In a shirt. Times have changed."

He stopped walking and so did I. "It's down to you," he said. He stooped, took my face in both of his big hands, and kissed me on the cheek. It was the kind of kiss you give a friend, but I felt the burn of his stubble and tried to imagine there was some passion in it. He smelled of sea air, clean and sharp.

I felt myself reach out a bit when he pulled away.

"It was nothing," I said. My heart was going fast and hard.

"You're incredible, Frances. When you arrived in Helmstown, I thought I knew why you'd come and what you were here for. But I didn't. You've changed me."

"Well," I said, trying — for God's sake — not to blush, "you've changed me, too."

"I'm afraid I probably have," he said. "But, look, I bought you a present."

He took out a thin box, which I recognized immediately from the gold royal seal. Berol Venus pencils.

"I'm sorry I broke the other ones," he said.

I took the pencils and smiled. For a messenger, a pencil is a gift of mixed feelings, but I did love my Venuses. And it felt good to get a present from Peter. I changed the subject so my pleasure wouldn't be too obvious.

"Has Rowenna said anything about you seeing Joe?" I asked.

"We talked briefly. She wants to take it slow, and she's not making any promises. I understand that. We have to go at Joe's pace. Rowenna says he's excited, but he's got used to What's-His-Name, and I've also got a bit of work to do, considering how long I've been away."

"It sounds like a good start, though," I said.

"I've been trying to tell myself not to get carried away, but it's so much better than I ever could have expected," he said.

We walked on down the sea path, into the strengthening wind, and two dogs approached us from behind. A gray whippet passed on one side of us and a huge gray Weimaraner on the other. It took me a moment to make the connection, but when I did, I turned around and looked back down the path to see Helen and Greg, hand in hand.

"Look," I said to Peter.

He turned. "Oh," he said. He was trying to look unimpressed, but I could see a little smile creeping through.

"We did that," I said.

"I suppose we did."

"Consequences. They're not all bad."

The dogs bounced on ahead of us, chasing each other and rearing with joy on their way to the undercliff path. I looked back again to see Helen bent over laughing as Greg said something to her.

"Anyway," Peter said, "you said you had something you needed to talk about."

"Oh, yeah. It's my brother. He's in a bad way, and I'm trying to work out how I can help him." I felt guilty as soon as I said it, like I'd ruined the happy mood.

Peter winced. It was an expression that said, *I feel for you and everything, but I've got a lot to do*. It was a new one for Peter. It wasn't new to me.

"It's all right," I said. "It'll be all right. I was going to go to the library, look up some stuff about the law. It's not the first time a bloke has accidentally hit another bloke too hard outside a pub. There must be other cases. I'm going to see if there's anything I can do."

There was the face again. Peter looked at his watch. "I'd really like to come with you, but I've got to get to this meeting."

"It's fine," I said. "I wasn't asking you to come."

I tried not to sound hurt, but it didn't work.

Up ahead, a police car pulled over and two officers got out. They walked onto the sea path, counted off the beach huts, and stopped at Peter's red door. We slowed our pace. "What's going on?" I said.

"Don't know," Peter said. "But I tell you what: you should go. Whatever they want, I'll handle it."

"OK."

"Come back later. About five-ish. We can talk about your brother then."

So I stopped and Peter walked on. The wind had picked up, and the air was like needles. I was standing near one of the seafront bars, where they'd hung those depressing old colored lightbulbs on a wire. I suppose they were trying to be retro and cool, this being Helmstown, where everything is retro and cool.

Peter reached the police officers, and they started to talk. From their body language, I could see that the policemen wanted to go into the hut, but Peter was shaking his head. One of the policemen took out a notebook, and as he did so, Peter turned quickly to me and made a gesture with his hand, a sort of wave that said, *Get gone.*

Just then, the wind took hold of two or three of the colored bulbs and smashed them against the wall of the bar. I flinched. Powdered red and blue glass swirled about on the ground, beneath the empty benches.

I got gone.

TWENTY-FIVE

In the library, I found plenty of cases of what the judges called "one-punch" deaths, most of them involving boxers or former boxers. None of them had happy endings.

A washed-up ex-pro, who'd never been as successful as his dad, smacked a bloke who had his hands in his pockets, in Yorkshire. Seven years for manslaughter.

A welterweight knocked a man down the steps of a London nightclub and then ran away to America. He said it was self-defense. Three years for manslaughter.

A young boxer, whom the judge described as a "predator," punched a man who was running away outside a bar in Birmingham. The verdict: murder, jailed for life.

The problem was that all the crimes were different, and all the men were different. And I couldn't help but think about the victims. The families. The injuries. Fractured eye socket, broken jaw, severe brain swelling. I felt sick. I looked down at my hand. Five thin fingers, a drawing bump on the middle one, graphite smudges on the skin from my pencils.

I took out the photo that Auntie Lizzie had given me: Johnny and me in the shed. It was just a ruined old shed in the middle of a disused field, really. I used to lie on Johnny's back while he did press-ups, and I'd watch the world go up and down. There were newspaper clippings of his career pinned up on the walls, and all these famous boxing quotes our granddad had copied out in red marker. Boxers talking about how they were in love with pain, addicted to their own hurt. There was also that quote by Mike Tyson about how he tries to punch the nose bone through his opponent's brain. That last one always disturbed me. It wasn't because I thought Johnny would ever try to do such a thing, but because there were people out there who would try to do that to Johnny. I'd *seen* them try to do it. And he was stupid enough to face up to them.

But there were also people out there, now, who thought Johnny was that type of man: a monster, a murderer. I prayed that the policeman he'd hit would pull out of his coma. That he would sit up and laugh. That he would remember throwing a punch at Johnny, admit to it, and they would make friends. They would play a game of chess together, for charity, as a protest against violence.

The only time I ever argued with Johnny was about boxing. Once I told a teacher, Miss O'Shea, about the Helmstown fight and how much it had upset me to see Johnny being hit. She said boxing was brutal and savage. I told Johnny, and he was furious. He said, "Your teacher doesn't understand. She's never had to fight for anything in her life. She doesn't understand what it means to be hungry."

"You mean angry?" I said.

Johnny took off his sunglasses. "I mean both," he said.

I thought of him doing press-ups in the shed. I thought of him sitting at the end of my bed when I had a fever, a pack of frozen peas on his swollen cheekbone, a pack of frozen carrots on my forehead. I thought of him hiding in some God-awful lonely part of England, running from ghosts and shadows.

He'd been trying to make a difference. He had this idea of running a boxing gym for kids. He wanted to call it the Top Gun Fight School. He'd done first-aid training and a course in fitness instruction. But none of that would ever happen now.

I pored over the definitions of manslaughter and murder in the legal textbooks. I couldn't make head nor tail of them. If you could prove that you were in such a messed-up mental state that you weren't like a normal human being, then you wouldn't be charged with murder.

Could it be argued that Johnny was different from "normal human beings"? That his father had beaten him, humiliated him? That he'd been a boxer — a job that involved being punched in the face every single day for ten years? Most people, when you throw a punch at them, will turn their back. It's a natural instinct for self-defense. Boxers have that instinct trained out of them. They are rewired, reprogrammed. Could I argue that Johnny had been turned into a machine?

But he did hit the guy. He knew what his hands were capable of, and he used them.

I heard Peter's voice in my head, imagined what he might have said. *Did your brother have a choice?* The truth was, I didn't know. I slammed the textbook shut. The other people in the library stared at me, but I stared back and, in turn, each of them looked away.

As planned, I went back to the beach hut at five p.m. I knocked and waited, wondering how Peter's meeting with Rowenna had gone. I thought of them staring at each other across the table in the hospital café and sighed. I knocked again. Nothing.

The air was full of water. Sea spray and summer rain. After a few more minutes, I decided to leave. *He's probably still with Rowenna and Ian,* I thought. *Probably just running late.* There was likely to be a perfectly good reason why he hadn't turned up to meet me. That's what I told myself, anyway.

TWENTY-SIX

I went back to the hut the next day and found him.

He was piling his stuff into a kit bag. He was not a good packer. All the paints and brushes—he just dumped them in. I watched him for a bit, puzzled. The sun was hanging unsteadily above the Big Dipper on Helmstown Pier.

"Hi," I said. "I figured it must have gone well yesterday, seeing as you didn't make it back for our meeting."

He froze, crouched, with his fingers around the straps of his bag. His green eyes flashed, and I couldn't decide if he looked more like a hunter or some poor creature scared out of its wits.

"What's the matter with you?" I said.

His limbs broke out of the freeze, and he stood up tall, looking both ways down the path. "Nothing," he said.

"So," I said, "how did it go? With Rowenna?"

"Great," he said. "They're going to let me take Joe out for the day. To the zoo."

"That's brilliant," I said. "Hey, it's been four days without any messages now. Do you think we've beaten it?"

"No," he said. "It's not as predictable as that." He couldn't even look at me. I knew there was something wrong, and although the day was warm, I shivered.

"Shall we go and get a cup of tea, then?" I said.

"I can't," he said.

"Why not?" I said. "Where are you going? You're acting weird. Even for *you*."

"I can't see you anymore, Frances," he said.

I felt the cold hard shock of his words.

"What are you talking about?" I said.

"Your uncle. Robert, is it?"

"What about him?" I said.

"He's had a word with the police."

I had almost forgotten about the two officers outside Peter's hut the day before.

"What do you mean?" I said.

"Apparently he's got friends in high places," Peter said. "The officers said they thought it was unwise for me to invite teenage girls into the hut. They made it sound like I was . . . *trying it on with you*. Which is crazy."

"Of course it is," I said.

I didn't think it was crazy. I'd have done anything to get him to try it on with me. Anything except ask.

"They seemed to know everything — well, not everything, but a lot. They said you were going through a tough time, with your brother's situation, and that your family thinks you're at risk."

"That's ridiculous," I said.

"They said that if I continued to hang around with you, they'd make sure I never saw my son again," he said. His voice was low and blank.

"What did you say?"

"I told them I'd leave you alone," he said.

"Right," I said. "But . . ."

What did I want to say? I wanted to say, *But surely you're not that weak. But surely you told them to stick it.*

"I mean, you do understand, don't you?" he said.

I nodded.

"Your uncle is a meddler," he said, and bent slowly to put some blank postcards into his bag. He looked nervously up and down the path again. I realized that he was hoping nobody would see us together.

"So that's it, is it?" I said.

"Well, not forever, obviously. Just until this thing with the police blows over. It's just—Joseph is my son, you know. I'd do anything for him."

"What about the recipients? What about the people we have to save? Am I supposed to work out my messages on my own?"

"You're good enough now. You can do it. And remember, Frances, you can't save everyone."

I shook my head. The question I really wanted to ask was this: *What about you and me?* But I didn't.

"Frances?" he said. "Tell me you understand. It's very important to me that you understand. *You're* important to me, as a friend. But I just can't have any contact with you for a while."

"I understand," I said flatly.

He hoisted his bag onto his shoulder and piled a few non-essentials into a box that he left on the grass behind the hut. Then he came back round and padlocked the front door. "I'll call you," he said.

I walked toward him, and I can honestly say that I was planning to kiss him. A kiss from a girl changes everything. It makes men stay when they say they're leaving. I'd seen it happen in films. And anyway, I desperately wanted to do it. I stared at his lips as I got closer. I stopped. We were so near to each other that I could feel his breath on me.

I kicked him in the shin as hard as I possibly could, and I ran.

I ran toward the sun without looking back. I knew the kick hadn't hurt him. He hadn't even flinched. He was strong. Physically.

I tried to drain myself with running. I tried to pour all of the energy and disappointment and fear out through my feet. I ran along the sea path, and then I went down the steps to the beach so I could hear the churning of the sea. The stones made me go slow. The last thing I remember about that morning was seeing the big rusty girders that held up the pier. Then I blacked out.

TWENTY-SEVEN

I must have lain on the beach for a long time. Eventually I staggered up onto street level, made my way onto the pier, and collapsed on a bench. The sea rolled in gently, and the rides and games pinged and whirled. I was numb, exhausted, but I tried to keep focused. I held the postcard in my hand, facedown, and had a good, stern word with myself. *Come on, Frances. You've got to look at it. There's no time for self-pity.*

It looked like a photograph. I couldn't believe I'd managed to draw something of such detail. It wasn't like any death scene I'd ever drawn, and it wasn't like any death scene Peter had ever painted.

It featured a man suspended in midfall above a pavement, his legs off the ground, his chin to his chest, an expression of pain on his face. He looked like he'd fallen into the drawing. Tiny grains of smashed glass surrounded him, like he'd just shaken water off his body. There was a lot of fine detail: the stubble on the man's face, the fields in the background, the shadow on the pavement. But there were hardly any clues.

Hardly anything to look at but the man, the glass, and the fields. He was in his early twenties. His hair was closely cropped; he wore a vest and jeans and big aviator sunglasses. Johnny.

Peter would've said it was inevitable, but I didn't believe in that.

I couldn't look at it for too long. My vision kept going gray, as if there were a part of my brain trying to turn out the lights because it didn't want my eyes to see the picture.

Pull yourself together, I thought. I tried to look for clues. Peter had taught me that there were always clues, even with a heart attack. But you could usually see more of the death scene — *the context*. This was too hard. Perhaps death was evolving again.

There was only one person who could have worked it out, of course, and that was Peter. But I didn't know where he was, and he wouldn't speak to me even if I did.

I had twenty-four hours to save my brother. I looked at my watch and could hardly believe the time — 4:30 p.m.

Twenty hours.

When you're in shock, you can force yourself to shut out the horror of a situation. It helps you to do what's necessary. That's where I was at. I had tunnel vision, and I wasn't thinking about anything but my next step.

By the time I reached the library, it had already closed. The Internet café didn't have the software I needed to zoom in on the picture, so I decided I'd have to do that when I got home. I took the postcard to the man at the desk.

"I need this photocopied, please," I said.

He looked at it and sighed. "Is this supposed to be art?"

"Just copy it," I said, sliding the money across the desk. He shrugged and did as I told him.

Outside, I started to get angry. I started to hate Peter for leaving me in this mess. I began to doubt that he was the person I thought he was. And yet I went back to the hut. The padlock glinted in the early evening light. The remaining box of his stuff was well hidden. I thought about throwing it in the sea, worthless as it was. Would he ever come back there? I didn't know. I set down my rucksack, took out a piece of paper and a Berol Venus, and I wrote.

Peter,

I know you don't want to see me, but this is serious. I blacked out and when I woke, I drew Johnny. I can't work out the message. I can't do it and I'm frightened. I can't find any clues.

I have less than a day to save my brother, and I don't even know where he is. I don't know where you are, either. I don't know where you live. You always said messengers should keep a low profile, but maybe you were just making sure you could dump me and run when it suited you. I need you now.

And not just because of Johnny.

I crossed out the last line until I tore through the paper, and then I slid the note, along with the copy of the drawing, halfway under the door and weighted them down with a rock. I imagined what it was like inside the beach hut. A dusty wooden void.

Maybe, I thought, I was to blame for what I'd drawn. Perhaps, deep in my mind, I wanted to find Johnny so much that I'd drawn him *on purpose*. But my inability to read the message just added to the frustration.

As I marched back to Auntie Lizzie's, I started to develop a plan of action. It was more a plan of desperation, really, but I had to try to kick-start my mind.

- Scan the photo, zoom in, and look for clues. What was happening in the picture? Where was it happening?
- Call Mum, call anyone who knew Johnny and might be able to guess where he would go at a time like this.
- Tomorrow: go to Hartsleigh very early and try to find Joe Davies. Even if he wouldn't tell me anything, he might accidentally lead me to Peter.

I told myself I could do it. I could figure it out. It was really just a question of following procedure. My self-assurance lasted about fifteen minutes, and by the time I got to Auntie Lizzie's house, I was a mess. The hope was draining out of me. My hands were shaking, and it felt like my throat was closing in. I was losing it. The sketch was in my rucksack, and I still had the pencil in my fist. I held it so tight that it felt like another bone in my hand. The drawing was, I suppose, just a few scratches on a postcard, but it had become the center of the world, and it was dragging everything — including me — toward it like a huge black hole.

I stood in the hallway with my back to the door and listened to the silence of the house. It was broken by footsteps on the stairs. They were quick and heavy, then they slowed, so I didn't need to look up to know that it was Uncle Robert.

"Hello, Frances," he said.

I glanced up at him, but I couldn't respond. The postcard, and what I had to do with it, filled my head so completely that there was barely even room for language. Uncle Robert stood there with his hands together. Auntie Lizzie emerged from the living room. "Hey," she said, her eyes cast down sympathetically. "Everything OK, love?"

"No," I said.

"We're sorry it had to come to this, but we really didn't know what else to do. You wouldn't talk to us, and we were worried," said Auntie Lizzie. She took a couple of steps toward me, but I didn't move.

"I spoke to my friend Brian, who works with the city police force," said Uncle Robert. "I asked his advice. That's all. About your friend —"

"Peter," I said quietly. What they were saying seemed so completely trivial, given what I had just drawn.

"Right. He's quite a bit older than you. Brian looked into things. We don't want to judge, but apparently Peter has had his problems. We didn't know if you knew. With his mental health and so forth."

I started to cry. I had kept my feelings under control for so long. I had been strong for my mum at home. I had been strong for Johnny, strong for Peter. But I was alone now, and I just couldn't do it anymore. I wasn't crying out of sadness or self-pity, though. It was fear.

"Oh, Fran, baby," said Auntie Lizzie. "I know it's hard." She put her arms around me and I began to shake.

"Johnny," I said through my tears.

"Johnny?" Auntie Lizzie said, slightly surprised. "Johnny will be OK, Fran."

"No," I gasped. "No."

"He will. We'll work something out," she said. "Robert knows a couple of people in law, and —"

I snapped. "You don't understand! You don't fucking know what's happening! He will *not* be OK! He's going to die! Johnny is going to die! Oh, Jesus. It's my fault. I have to . . ."

I turned and opened the door, but Auntie Lizzie kept hold of my arm, and pretty soon Uncle Robert had hold of me, too.

"Let me go!" I screamed. "I have to go! I've got to *do* something!"

Uncle Robert was stronger than I would have thought. He had me around the middle, and I couldn't break free. I knew I'd completely lost control, because Auntie Lizzie and Uncle Robert stopped talking to me and spoke to each other instead. *"Have you got her?" "Yes. Close the door." "Should we call someone?" "Let's get her upstairs, give her a chance to calm down."*

"For God's sake, let me go!" I screamed.

It was all a bit hazy after that.

TWENTY-EIGHT

When I woke, it was already morning. My head felt heavy and my mouth dry. The room was a shambles. There were clothes everywhere; the bedside lamp was smashed, the glass from the bulb all over the floor, and the curtains had been dragged off the pole. I must have really lost it.

I looked at the clock. It was past ten. Disaster. I had less than two and a half hours. I put on my jeans and T-shirt and ran into the hallway. Auntie Lizzie was standing there with a glass of juice. She looked like she'd hardly slept.

"Are you OK?" she said. Her voice was low, serious, worried.

"Yeah. I'm fine. Thank you," I said.

"You were in a bad state."

"I'm sorry about the mess," I said.

She shrugged. "We got you to calm down a bit, then gave you some sleeping tablets. Here, drink some fluids. It's lime cordial, like you used to have at Nana's when you were small."

I took the glass. It occurred to me suddenly that since I hadn't delivered the message, then someone might be starting to feel very sick right now. "Christ," I said under my breath.

"Frances, what's wrong?" Auntie Lizzie said.

"Nothing. Nothing's wrong with *me*. How about you? You're not unwell?" I stared at her closely, checked her eye whites and her lips.

"I'm fine, Frances, what are you talking about?"

"What about Max? Is he OK?"

"Yes. He's playing video games. He's going to keep you company while I sort out some breakfast downstairs."

"Keep me company . . ." I said. She obviously meant *guard me*. "Listen, I *really* need to go out. It's . . . it's very important that I speak to . . . certain people."

"We just can't let you go, Frances. You are clearly feeling unwell. You weren't rational last night. It would be wrong of us to allow you to leave the house."

I kept hold of my temper. I knew that the angrier I got, the harder it would be to get out. I sighed. "Right," I said.

"That's my girl. You're going to be just fine. You need to rest," she said, and kissed my cheek.

I went back into my room and tried to think. My loved ones were supposed to get sick if I didn't deliver the message, but who *were* my loved ones? Auntie Lizzie and Max were fine. Maybe, I thought for a second, Peter, who had now become my closest friend, but I dismissed that idea.

Fragments of conversations with Peter came back, and suddenly it became clear. I was in the double bind, just as Peter had been with Tabby. Johnny was the person closest to me, and Johnny was the recipient. So if I delivered the message, he'd die, and if I didn't, he'd die anyway.

What was I going to do?

At least if I could get to him and deliver the message, I would have a chance of saving him. If I just sat there and let it all happen, he was doomed.

I tried to direct my energy toward getting out of that soft, plush prison. I stuck my head out into the hall and listened. Auntie Lizzie was in the kitchen, so both the front and back doors would be in her line of sight. In any case, I was aware that even if I got out of the house, I still didn't know where Johnny was or how I was supposed to get there.

My mouth was dry, so I gulped down half of the lime cordial in the bedroom. The nostalgic taste was painful. I wished I was a little girl again. How much would I alter if I could go back? I shook my head. There was still a chance, however small, that I could change what was happening *now*.

I took the message out of my rucksack and stared at my brother's face. I saw how it had changed since I'd last seen him. He looked wasted and weak in the picture, like he hadn't been eating. But there were no further clues.

I looked up at Peter's painting of the boat, which I'd leaned against the wall on the bedside table. I remembered what he'd written at the bottom. *Just because something is off to the side doesn't mean it's not the point.*

I looked back down at the message and tried to ignore Johnny. In the background, I saw a figure. It was a man, but he was too far away to see any telling details without scanning and zooming the image. I let my eyes wander over the wire fence behind Johnny. I let them wander over the fields behind the fence. I had the uncanny feeling, suddenly, that I knew the shape of those hills. It was as if my recent dreams had spilled over into real life. And then I saw it, way off in the distance: his shed. His old shed on Nana's land, just as it had appeared so many times in my mind these past few weeks. He was somewhere in Whiteslade.

I went over to the window. If I was quiet, I could drop down onto the garage roof. I took hold of the window sash, but it was locked. They'd barricaded me in. "Let me out!" I shouted, and I heard footsteps on the landing. I was becoming delirious again. I needed to calm down.

I picked up my phone and dialed Peter. It went straight to voice mail. "Please, Peter," I said. "Please call me. I can't get out of here. It's Whiteslade. My brother is in Whiteslade. He doesn't have long. You know what, Peter? After everything I did for you—I hate you for this."

There was a knock at the door. I hung up. "What?"

Max came in. He seemed shaken. He sat on the bed, holding a console and his kendo mask. "Do you want to play some games?" he said.

"Games? Bloody games? I don't have time, Max!" I said angrily. He looked petrified. I had sort of forgotten that he was younger than me.

"I'm sorry, Max. It's just that I need to get out of here, and nobody is listening to me."

191

"OK," he said.

"Have you been sent in here to be the new prison guard?" I said.

He nodded.

"Max," I said, realizing that he was probably my only hope, "can you help me get out of here?"

He winced. "Look, Mum said you're not feeling too good. I don't want to do anything that puts you in danger."

"I need to get out!" I shouted. He flinched and I lowered my voice. "Can you answer my questions? Can you at least do that?"

"Nothing wrong with answering questions, I suppose," he said sadly.

I was about to ask him where the key to the window was, but I changed my tactic at the last moment, knowing that he wouldn't tell me. Not yet.

"Do *you* think I'm mad, too?" I asked.

He took off his glasses and rubbed his eyes, which looked small without the magnification of the spectacle lenses. "I've certainly thought about it," he said quietly.

"What did you decide?"

He stared away from me.

"What if I told you that Johnny was in danger?" I said. "Do you think that's a crazy thing to say?"

"No. It's obvious Johnny's in danger. He's on the run."

"OK, what if I told you I knew how to save him? What would you think then?"

"I don't know."

I hadn't seen him like this. He was never a chirpy lad, but he usually had a calmness about him. That was gone. The thought arose, fleetingly, that he might be worried about me.

"You haven't answered my first question. Do you think I'm mad?"

"There's plenty of evidence to say that you are," he said. "It's not only that you smashed the room up. It's more the other stuff. First you're trying to stop some woman who doesn't even know you from getting drunk, then you're looking after eleven-year-old boys at the skate park. What's it all about, Frances?"

"My dad always said you should try to do good whenever you can," I said instinctively.

"Did he?" Max said.

"No," I said. "My brother said it, actually."

Max thought for a moment. "Well, if you're crazy, then as far as I can see, it's making you do the right thing all the time. You're pretty much my hero at the moment."

I nearly broke down. "Bless you, Maxi," I said.

His shoulders sank back into place now, as if he'd made a decision. The old Max was back.

"Any more questions?" he said.

"If you needed to get to Whiteslade and you had . . ." I looked at my watch. "Jesus. And you had an hour and a half, and no car, what would you do?"

"Whiteslade? Like, near Nana's old house? God, that's a bit remote. Well, I'd probably steal my dad's Vespa."

"Your dad has a *motor scooter*?" I said.

"Of course he does," Max said.

"And can you ride it?" I said.

"Theoretically."

Perfect. I grabbed my rucksack, put the message inside, and turned to the window.

"Dammit," I said. "And how might you get out of the window if it happened to be locked and the key was nowhere to be seen?"

"I'd probably check under the wardrobe," he said, standing from the bed.

I retrieved the key and stood. He smiled. "Shall we?" he said.

The Vespa was in the garage, under a dust sheet. It was sky blue, with fancy silver letters. I couldn't help the tiny voice in my head saying, *Uncle Robert—what a poseur*. Max looked at the scooter and bit his lip—he knew he was going to get in trouble, but he didn't say anything about it.

"There's only one helmet," he said.

"You take it," I said.

"No way," he said. "Someone's got to look after you. Besides, I've got this." He put a kendo mask on over his glasses. "Bought it in the sale."

I put on the blue helmet and looked at my watch. The thought occurred to me that we might not get there in time, that I might be on my way to find my brother's body. I shook the thought off.

Max was shaky on the scooter at first, but he soon got the

hang of it, zipping through the city traffic onto the coastal road, past the backs of the beach huts. I looked at Peter's and the square of flattened grass where his final box of possessions had been. He'd really gone.

We went through Crowdean, past the retirement home, with its painful memories, and out toward Whiteslade. The scenery changed, became more farmish. The towns unraveled. I started to recognize the potholed roads from when I was a kid, when Nana was alive, but it all looked so small now. Overgrown hedges clambered over random little houses. There was a run-down high street with charity shops and a couple of cafés. There were more Saint George flags in the windows here. More patriots, although one lone house had an Italian tricolor draped over the veranda.

I couldn't see the shed up on the hills behind, and even if I could, how was I going to find the street where Johnny was to die? The sun was bright and mean. I tapped Max on the shoulder and gestured that he should pull over and park the scooter.

It was almost noon, and nothing looked familiar. How many square meters in a place like Whiteslade? Too many. He could have been anywhere. I walked in one direction and then spun round and ran in another, but I was just guessing. Max followed me, and he looked more and more disturbed.

"Frances, are you OK? Can you explain what we're doing?"

I held my head. "We're . . . we're looking for Johnny. . . . I need to sit down."

We found a bench next to a telephone box. "Think," I said to myself. I took the postcard out of my rucksack and stared at it again.

"What's that?" Max said.

God knows what he could see when he looked at it. He probably thought it was an abstract art print from the local museum. "Max, I'm trying to find a street, but all the streets look the same here. You see that den—the small ruin on the hill?"

He turned around. "Yeah."

"That's my only landmark. But you can see it from every damn street in the village. I think Johnny might have been hiding there."

"So why don't we just go there, then?" he said.

"I'm afraid that I'll miss him. He's going to be somewhere down here in . . ." I looked at my watch. "He's going to be here very soon anyway." I put the postcard down on the bench and put my head in my hands.

Max took off his glasses, laid them on the bench, and rubbed his eyes. He'd put the left lens of the spectacles over the postcard. The image was magnified. Johnny's face had expanded. I picked up the glasses and moved them like a spyglass to focus more clearly. There was something—some detail—reflected in the lenses of Johnny's aviators.

I couldn't see it clearly, but it was all I'd got—my last hope.

"Max, was there an Internet café on the high street?"

"I think so."

"Let's go."

He didn't move, and I could see he was thinking he'd made the wrong decision. He was thinking that I was crazy after all, and that he was going to get into serious trouble about the scooter.

I kissed him on the forehead. "Max. Thank you for coming with me. Maybe you were right. Maybe one of us should walk up to the den. Why don't you go?"

I knew Johnny wouldn't be there, but I'd involved Max too much already. I had to do this alone. He looked up at the den.

"Take a little walk, eh?" I said.

"OK," he said. "If you're sure you'll be all right. I'll meet you back here."

I barged into the Internet café and sat at a machine. I was frantic now, shouting at the computer to load. People were looking over, but I didn't care. I scanned in the postcard and it came up. I scrolled along and caught the figure in the distance that I'd noticed that morning. It was a policeman running toward Johnny. They'd found him. They'd chased him. Maybe it was the police that caused his death. It was hard for me to zoom in on Johnny's face, but I had to do it. I could see the shock in him, his mouth open. I went up to the lenses of his aviators, hoping to God for some clue to where he was.

There *was* a clue to his location, but that wasn't what I noticed first. What I noticed first was the reflection of another man crumpled at the waist, cruelly twisted, and sprawled across the bonnet of a light-colored car. There was no doubt who it was.

Peter.

I raised my hands to my head. What was happening? It took me a moment to work it out. The message wasn't for Johnny at all. It was for Peter. I kept thinking. In my mind, I saw the flattened square of grass behind his hut. He'd been back there, which meant he'd probably found the note and the copy of the picture. He'd surely have looked at the picture. Without either of us knowing it, I'd delivered his death message.

TWENTY-NINE

I looked back at the image. Why was Johnny in the picture? Why were they together? The glass around my brother was from the car, I could see that now. I could also see, in the reflected surface of Johnny's sunglasses, a house across the street. It had a flag draped over the veranda. A tricolor. Italian.

I ran out of the café without paying. The man at the till shouted after me, but I barely heard him. I heard sirens. I ran through the grid of little streets and went past the bench on which I'd just been sitting. I stopped. Someone was sitting there and at first I thought it was Maxi, but it wasn't. It was Joe. He looked dazed.

"Oh. It's you," he said.

"What the hell are *you* doing here?" I said.

"I don't know," he said. "We've been to the zoo and he's supposed to be taking me home, but my . . . Peter's acting really weird. He . . . he got a voice mail on his phone, and he said we had to turn around and come here, wherever *here* is."

"Don't move," I said.

I kept running, and as I came to the street with the Italian flag, I saw the policeman running toward me from the end of the road. I stopped and looked around, but there was no sign of anyone else. I was shaking.

It happened so quickly that I barely had time to think. I can separate each movement now, of course, not that it makes any difference. This is what I saw and heard:

A light-colored car came hurtling around the corner from behind me, doing at least fifty.

A man in a vest, sunglasses, and jeans burst out of an alleyway halfway down the street and sprinted across the road. My brother. I barely had time to feel the emotions that came with seeing him after so long.

Peter Kennedy emerged from the same alley a split second later, chasing Johnny, and being followed by another uniformed police officer.

Until the last moment, it seemed that the car would hit Johnny, but in that tenth of a second, everything changed. Peter changed it. He pushed Johnny onto the pavement and tried to evade the front end of the car. The driver hit the brakes, but he was way too late and Peter was thrown over the bonnet.

I screamed and began to run. The car stopped up ahead, leaving its black trails of rubber on the gray tarmac. The two policemen converged on the scene. I thought one of them would come over to arrest Johnny, but they both went to Peter, who was lying in the middle of the road.

I went to Johnny. He looked up at me. His clothes were

covered in sparkling blue glass, and his arm was raw and bleeding.

"Fran?" he said. He had no idea what was happening.

"Johnny," I said. "You're OK."

He looked at the two policemen crouching beside Peter. I ran over to them, but I knew. I knelt down by Peter's body, by his face, and I tried to talk to him. His eyes were closed. I can't remember what I said, whether I said thank you or sorry. I only know that he didn't respond.

Johnny had gone over to the car and was talking to the driver. "What the hell were you doing, mate?" he was saying. "Mate? Can you hear me?"

One of the policemen looked up. "You wait there, you!" he shouted to Johnny.

Johnny was going nowhere. He was going to be fine. But Peter was not.

THIRTY

I've been over it so many times. Part of being a messenger is imagining other people's lives. I try every day to re-create the last hours of Peter Kennedy from any bit of information I can gather. I have talked to Joe — although God knows he didn't want to talk to me. I have talked to Johnny, the police officers, and the paramedics. There was nothing they could do to save Peter.

You cannot know everything about a moment in time. It's impossible. You can't be certain about the thoughts and motives of the people involved, but you can make a decent guess.

Peter took his son to the zoo in a car he'd hired that morning. Joe was nervous to begin with and was still limping because of his sprained ankle, but the antics of the lemurs made them both laugh, and that relaxed them. Before lunchtime, they set off for Hartsleigh. Peter was happy, but in a curious way. It was as though the happiness wasn't really his. It was like he was borrowing the good feeling, and he had a nagging sensation of unfinished business. Nevertheless, he and Joe drove back along the coastal road, politely sharing information about their lives.

As they went through Helmstown, Peter stopped to pick up his final box of belongings from the beach hut, being careful to make sure that a teenage girl wasn't waiting for him. He checked the padlock and noticed the piece of paper and the postcard under his door.

He looked at them on his way back to the car. He didn't know how long he had to figure out the image. He resolved to drop Joe off, go home, and put the postcard through his scanner. But after a few more minutes on the road, his phone beeped. He hadn't heard it ring. It was in the coin tray.

"You've got a voice mail," Joe said.

Peter picked it up.

"You shouldn't do that while you're driving, you know," Joe said anxiously.

"It's all right," Peter said. "I'm being careful."

He listened to the voice mail, checked his mirrors, and then spun the car around. He headed for Whiteslade.

"Where are we going?" Joe said.

"I've got to do something. Won't take long."

He happened to be following the police van into Whiteslade and so he saw it pull over. The officers got out—one started to chase Johnny while the other went around the block in an attempt to cut him off. Johnny ran straight past Peter's car. Peter pulled over and got out with the copy of the message, quickly giving some money to his son and telling him to go to the shops.

Peter was quick on his feet. Quicker than an anxious,

sleepless, out-of-shape boxer who'd been living rough. He hadn't had time to study the message properly, hadn't realized it was meant for him, and as he ran down that alley, he had no idea what was going to happen.

That's my latest version. Some days I change certain details. Some days I imagine that Peter was angry with me for some reason. Sometimes I make him more loving. I make him miss me. The only bit I can't change, of course, is the ending.

There are consequences, the old Peter would probably have said. An unstoppable, inevitable chain. He might have said that he and Johnny had been on a collision course since the day they were born. That Johnny was on the run because he'd punched a policeman, that he'd only punched a policeman because he'd trained as a boxer, that he'd only trained as a boxer because he'd done so badly at school, that he'd done so badly at school because his father abused him. The old Peter would have said that there are some things — some people — you just can't help.

But Peter changed.

There's only one person to blame, as far as I'm concerned. I served Peter with the message of his death. Not only that, but I convinced him he could make a difference. I convinced him he could save people from a fate he thought was inevitable. That's why he went after Johnny. That's why he died.

I've never believed in fate, inevitability. I believe we *can* change things. And so I have to take responsibility. It was me. I led him to his death. It was my fault. I was the messenger.

* * *

It's easier to know what that day was like for Johnny, because a week later he told me, during one of the many visits I made to him in police custody. After the car that hit Peter stopped, Johnny went over and discovered that the driver was a man in his late sixties. He'd been driving erratically because of a tightness in his chest. He was trying to get home so he could take some painkillers and ask his wife, a nurse, what was going on.

Johnny asked the guy what the hell he thought he was doing, but the man couldn't reply. He couldn't get his breath. Soon he went pale and lost consciousness. He was having a heart attack.

Johnny had done a first-aid course. He dragged the man from the car and resuscitated him in the middle of the road. The paramedics said he'd saved the man's life, but Johnny doesn't want to talk about it.

"It's all very well, what I did for the bloke in the car, but that other guy died because of me, Frances."

He's talking about Peter, of course, although I've never told him who Peter was. Maybe I will, one day.

While Johnny was on the run, the policeman he'd punched began to recover consciousness. It turns out waking from a coma isn't like they show it in the movies. You don't just sit up, tanned and fit, and start jabbering away to your beautiful wife. The guy woke up gradually, surfacing for a few minutes at a time, and then going back under. When he eventually came out of the coma for good, he was confused and upset. Even now, he's still struggling. He's having trouble with the vision in one eye, but his speech is fully restored. He's alive.

Johnny's never met him, but there's talk that it could happen, at some point, when Johnny gets out.

My brother accepted his short prison sentence gratefully. The landlord of the pub outside of which he hit the policeman found some temporarily misplaced CCTV footage showing the guy throwing the first punch. The judge said Johnny probably acted in self-defense, but that he knew the sort of damage he was capable of. Running away didn't do him any favors, either.

Just as the policeman's recovery has been gradual, so will Johnny's be. He's cheeked the prison staff a few times. Interestingly, he's abandoned his idea of a youth boxing gym. You know what he's teaching the other convicts? Freestyle skipping. Apparently it's catching on. It's good for your heart, and nobody gets their face smashed in. "I can't rub out the bad things I've done," Johnny said last time I visited. "But I can scribble some good ones over the top."

I told Johnny that I knew the stories about our dad were lies. I told him it didn't matter, because just having Johnny tell me the stories was enough. He could have been talking about a rare species of pig, for all I cared. I got more than the father I deserved. I got Johnny.

Initially, Joe Davies didn't want anything to do with me, but he is coming round. When I visit Helmstown, me and Max take him to the skate park. Max is rubbing off on him, which can only be a good thing. For a while, I suspect Joe thought it would have been better never to have met his father, but I'm doing my best to fill in some gaps. I tell him stories about Peter, and while I gloss over some of the details, I never lie.

Me? Well, I'm a messenger, aren't I? It was my hope, when I came home, that what happened in Helmstown would stay in Helmstown. But then I blacked out in the new shopping center back home, woke up, and drew a poor lad from the college, lying at the bottom of a high-security multistory car park. There is a sign above the entrance to that car park saying that it's one of the three safest places in Europe.

I caught up with the boy on the steps as he was walking up to the top floor, his head hanging. His girlfriend had left him for an older man, he said.

"How old is he?" I said.

"Seventeen," he said.

"So what you going to do?" I said, noticing his good broad shoulders.

"I'm gonna chuck meself off the roof."

"You're not," I said.

"I am. What you gunna do about it?" he said. It was nice to hear the local accent again.

"I'll do whatever it takes," I said. "I'll *kiss* you if I have to."

He frowned, because he was a bit surprised. Then I could see his mind working, wondering if he could bargain with me, get more than a kiss. Sam, his name is. Scribble over the bad stuff with good.

* * *

I've had to get my act together. Filing systems, phone books, a laptop. My drawing is clearer, sharper, and death has not evolved any further, for now. Sometimes I want to tell the people I save: *Use this time—this extra time is for you! Do something special with it.*

I don't, of course. Even if they believed me, the world is a fragile place, and you don't want too many folk living each day like it's their last. It'd be chaos.

Besides, there are some deaths you just have to accept. I have made messages of elderly people in hospital. They're in pain. There's not much you can do except bring the messages. I mean, I can't cure cancer. My hope is that one day I'll save someone who can. Sometimes you save someone who was going to be murdered, and they get murdered anyway. Sometimes you save someone, and they go on to do something bad. But I always save them if I can. In spite of everything that has happened, I still have got to believe that people can change. Otherwise, what's the point?

I know one day I'll see someone give me that same look I gave Peter, and that I'll have to teach them the messenger ways. It'll be nice to have some company. I don't know what I'll tell them, though. I try to stay positive. Maybe I'll tell them we're not really messengers of death. Perhaps we're just here to save a few lucky ones. To change a few things for the better. This thing—this power that I have—it drew me to Peter.

So maybe it's a gift, after all.

ACKNOWLEDGMENTS

I would like to thank the following people for helping me with this book: Mara Bergman, Véronique Baxter, Emily Hahn, Julie Redfern, and John Paul Temple, who taught me about boxing. Thanks also to Arts Council England.